THE HEX FACTOR

FACTOR

Dark Tide

To Mum

STRIPES PUBLISHING
An imprint of Little Tiger Press
1 The Coda Centre, 189 Munster Road
London SW6 6AW

A paperback original
First published in Great Britain in 2013

Text copyright © Harriet Goodwin, 2013
Cover copyright © Stripes Publishing Ltd, 2013
Inside illustrations copyright © Richard Allen, 2013

ISBN 978-1-84715-381-4

Printed and bound in the UK.

10 9 8 7 6 5 4 3 2 1

THE HEX FACTOR
Dark Tide

Harriet Goodwin

Stripes

1.
Saul's Message

Mrs Fox sipped her coffee and glanced down at the local paper.

"Looks like they've finally got permission to build that new multiplex in the centre of town," she said. "I bet you and your friends will be pleased about that, Xanthe."

Xanthe nodded over her bowl of cereal.

"Oh, and it says here the park's re-opening today," her mother went on. "The area surrounding the boathouse is still roped off, but the café's open and most of the path round the lake." She looked up from the paper. "Ten days since it happened and they're still no closer to tracking down the person responsible. You'd think the police would have made an arrest by now, wouldn't you?"

"Er, I guess so," murmured Xanthe, flushing. She finished her cereal and busied herself with a slice of toast.

Mrs Fox let out a long sigh. "I've probably said this a hundred times, but I'm so glad you were with your great-grandmother that day. I know how much you and Grace love it down at the park. The idea that you could have been there doesn't bear thinking about. Does it, Robert?" She nudged her husband. "*Robert?* Are you listening to a word I'm saying?"

Her husband looked up absently from his own newspaper. "Sorry? Were you talking to me?"

"I was *saying*," said Mrs Fox, "that they still haven't caught the person who set fire to the boathouse."

"There might not be anyone to catch," replied Mr Fox. "The police haven't ruled out the possibility that it might just have been a terrible accident."

His wife rolled her eyes.

"Oh, come on! What about the lake? They found holes in the ice, remember? And footprints on the jetty. Something very odd was going on down there that day. Something very odd indeed."

"Well, if they haven't caught anyone by now, I shouldn't think they ever will," said Mr Fox, helping himself to more coffee. He returned to his newspaper. "Seems the weather's been causing havoc over the weekend. Some parts of the country have seen more rain than they usually do in a month."

Xanthe yawned. What was it with grown-ups and the weather? Sometimes it seemed like it was all they ever talked about. And why did they need to read about it in the newspaper when you only needed to look out of the window to see what was going on? Still, it was better than listening to her mum rabbit on about the boathouse fire. Every time *that* subject was mentioned she just wanted the floor to open up and swallow her.

Her father shook out the paper. "Flood alerts remain in place throughout the country," he read. "The authorities in London are particularly concerned about rising water levels in the Thames. However, with the rain now easing off, it's hoped there will soon be an improvement in the situation."

Mrs Fox laughed. "This country never *has* been able to cope with a bit of rain," she said. "At least Milchester hasn't been too badly affected. Just a couple of road closures down by the library. Apart from that we seem to have got off pretty lightly." She turned her attention to Xanthe. "What've you got on at school today? Anything interesting?"

Xanthe pulled a face. "Just normal lessons this morning," she said. "Though Miss Ambrose said she was planning something for English, so maybe it won't *all* be boring. Oh, and we've got art this afternoon. I expect we'll be carrying on with our project on human expressions." She got to her feet, still munching her toast.

"What's the hurry?" asked Mrs Fox, looking at her watch. "You've got plenty of time before the bus."

Xanthe shrugged. "I could do with a bit of time to myself before school, that's all."

Her father peered at her over the paper.

"Time to yourself?" he teased. "Haven't you had enough of that? Apart from a visit to your great-grandmother's, you've been holed up in your bedroom all weekend." He grinned. "You've pretty much morphed into a teenager overnight!"

"No, I haven't! It's just that I've – well, I've had loads of homework to do."

Mr Fox winked at her. "I'm not complaining. It's great to see you taking your studies so seriously. Besides, after that cold you had last week, it's probably a very good thing you've had a nice quiet weekend at home."

Xanthe nodded but said nothing. It was hardly surprising she'd had a cold. Given that she'd spent the best part of ten minutes in a freezing lake a few days earlier, it was a miracle she hadn't come down with anything more serious.

And as for Dad thinking she'd had a nice quiet weekend – well, if only he knew.

Xanthe closed her bedroom door and sat down at her desk.

Slipping her hand into her skirt pocket, she took out her locket and held the battered oval of silver up by its chain, twisting it round until she could see the faded shape of the letter E engraved into the back of its casing. She opened the lid and ran her finger over the smooth piece of moonstone inside. It didn't matter how often she looked at it, the sight of that milky-white crystal always made her tingle with pride. It made her feel safe, too. As long as she had the locket and moonstone with her, she knew she could defend herself.

She put the locket back in her pocket and stared straight ahead, focusing all her attention on an imaginary point on the wall in front of her. Surely she would see one today. She'd spent the whole weekend practising.

It wasn't as if she didn't know what she was looking for. She'd seen one twice before: the first in maths on the morning of her thirteenth birthday, when the multiplication sign on her test paper had glowed bright red, and the second in science, when the strange shape had appeared on the piece of metal Saul was dropping into a test tube of acid. Both times

9

the results had been pretty spectacular, and both times the glowing Xs had simply appeared before her eyes. But that was because the person sparking them had been in the same room as her. Now she was attempting to pick up a hex from far away.

She concentrated even harder, forcing herself to block out the clattering of cups and plates coming from the kitchen below.

Filter out the distractions. That was what Grandma Alice had told her. *Filter out all the outside noise and concentrate on the job in hand. You won't pick up a faraway hex if your mind's on other things.*

Not that her great-grandmother expected her to see anything yet. Apparently it was still too early to be picking up long-distance hexes.

Xanthe sat back in her chair and sighed.

It was no good. It just wasn't going to happen. Perhaps she needed a break. She'd spent most of the weekend like this, sitting at her desk staring into space when she could have been going out with her friends instead. And all the while her parents had thought she'd been getting on with her homework.

She eyed her school bag. Her maths textbook was poking out of the top, as if to remind her of all the work she hadn't done. She'd have to try and do some of it on the bus – the last thing she wanted was to get on the wrong side of Miss Pimm again. At least her teacher had apologized for blaming her for the rude remark scrawled at the bottom of her maths test, but there was no way she was going to risk any more upset.

Xanthe looked up at the ceiling. She couldn't help feeling a tiny bit guilty that Kelly had ended up taking the blame for everything, when Donna had been the real culprit. It wasn't like Kelly had had anything to do with the incidents in maths and science. But she'd set off the fire alarm, hadn't she? She hadn't been completely innocent. *A nasty little troublemaker*, that's how Saul had described her. A troublemaker and a creep.

Her face broke into a grin. Saul. At least that was something that was going in the right direction. Ever since her party she'd been hoping he might finally get round to asking her out, and as of last night things were definitely looking more hopeful.

They'd had this amazing dance at the party: close enough to send electric shocks through her entire body. Of course, it had been a nightmare at school on the Monday. Whenever they'd gone anywhere near one another someone had made an embarrassing comment. Some of the boys had even started wolf-whistling at them. In the end it had been easier simply to keep their distance. To make matters worse, they hadn't even been able to text each other:

though Saul didn't know it, his mobile was sitting somewhere at the bottom of the lake in the park, and so far he hadn't got a replacement.

Then last night, just as she'd been about to settle down to a bit more concentration practice, she'd had a text from him. *Got a new phone AT LAST*, it read. *Want to meet up after school sometime this week?*

She had hugged herself with excitement. When she'd recovered enough to think straight, she'd tried out about ten different replies in her head before deciding on something that would do. *Sure. Which day?* she'd texted back, hoping she sounded keen but not desperate. She'd never spent so long wondering what to say to him in the old days: before the party they had texted each other all the time with funny little anecdotes or about TV programmes they'd watched.

A few minutes later her mobile had beeped once again. *Tuesday's good for me. What about you?*

Tuesday's fine, she'd replied, though a lot of other adjectives had been whirling round her head. Tuesday would, in fact, be awesome, brilliant, super-cool.

Xanthe thought of the small blue box lying in the bottom drawer of her desk. Inside it was a pair of amber earrings: Saul's birthday present to her. It was hard to know which meant more to her: the locket or the earrings. She hoped she'd never have to choose between them.

He'd given her a card, too: not a jokey one like most of the others had given her, but a really nice art print. Inside it he'd written, *To Xanthe, Have the best birthday ever, Love Saul.* There it was in black and white. The L word. It still made her heart lurch to read it. She'd hidden the card in the drawer with the earrings, because she didn't want anyone else reading it: especially not her parents. For now it would be her little secret. After all, she was getting pretty good at those.

From the same drawer, Xanthe took out the slim gold notebook she had got on her birthday as a diary. She'd had it less than two weeks, but already she couldn't imagine being without it. Apart from talking to Grandma Alice, it was the only way she could get things off her chest.

Shaking out her bunch of keys, she selected the smallest one and slid it into the lock at the side of the diary.

There on the front page was the first entry, written on the day her great-grandmother had told her everything: *Friday, 10th January*, it read. *Today I found out that I am a witch.*

Xanthe allowed herself a small smile. That day seemed like a lifetime ago, though in fact it was less than a fortnight. Since then so much had happened: the surprise meeting with Donna beside the boathouse, when her classmate had revealed that it was *she* who was the Hexing Witch – not Kelly; their fall through the ice; the discovery that she could breathe underwater; and then the moment just after Donna had hexed her, when she had summoned fire in her defence, like the first True Witch had done over a thousand years before. *To think you defended yourself just as Ethelfreda did*, Grandma Alice had said, when Xanthe had arrived at her house later on that afternoon, dripping wet and shivering with cold. *I can't get over how brilliant you've been.*

Xanthe flushed with pleasure at the memory of those words.

Her eyes flitted over the entries she had made since. She'd certainly done a good job of covering the creamy white sheets. Some of it was neat, written as she sat at her desk, trying to make sense of the bombshell that had changed her life forever, but there were other bits she could hardly read. Those were the entries she had made in the middle of the night when she had woken with her brain teeming, desperate to get the thoughts out of her exploding head and on to the page.

The last entry had been written on Friday, not long after she'd got home from school.

Weird day, it read. *Donna is seriously freaking me out. She's been really quiet all week, hardly saying a word to anyone, but today there was something different about her. I sneaked a glance at her in the lunch queue, and she looked really pleased with herself. It was as if she was hugging something to herself. And then I saw her outside the gates after school talking into her mobile, nodding and smiling.* After this she had drawn a sad face. *WHAT IS SHE UP TO?* the diary entry went on. *Is she plotting something? Wish I knew whether or not she's told her ancestor about what happened between us. Maybe too embarrassed. HOPE SO.*

Xanthe tried to ignore the sick feeling rising from the pit of her stomach. Donna had certainly been acting very strangely last Friday. Instead of looking haunted and ashamed, as she had done earlier in the week, she seemed to be brimming over with excitement and self-confidence. Honestly, it was a nightmare being at the same school as a Hexing Witch.

She picked up a pencil from her desk and started to write.

Monday, 20th January. Still not picking up any hexes. Starting to feel like the whole thing might have been a dream, and that I don't have any stupid powers. She sucked the end of the pencil. *Really worried about Donna, too. Something's definitely going on.*

She snapped the diary shut at the sound of her

mother's voice calling from the bottom of the stairs. "Xanthe! You'll be late for the bus!"

Xanthe locked the diary and slid it back inside the drawer.

"Coming!" she shouted.

She checked her skirt pocket once more for her locket, then put on her coat and picked up her school bag.

One way or another, it was going to be an interesting week.

2.
Macbeth

Xanthe stuffed her maths homework back into her bag and scrambled off the bus just before it pulled away from Milchester High.

That had been a bit close. Another few seconds and she would have missed her stop. She was going to have to organize herself a lot better than this.

Hurrying in through the school gates, she came face to face with Kelly. For a moment the two girls stared at one another, Kelly's lips twitching as she fought back a snide comment. Xanthe held her breath. It had been like this all last week. But Kelly hadn't once opened her mouth and said anything. After the trouble she'd been in at the start of term, she couldn't afford to put a foot wrong.

Xanthe did a neat little side-step and walked off,

scouring the playground for Grace.

Her best friend came rushing up to her. "Xanthe! We missed you at the cinema on Saturday. Everyone was there."

Xanthe put down her school bag and gave Grace a hug. "Everyone?"

"If you mean Saul, yes. He was asking where you were."

"I wish I could have come," sighed Xanthe. "But I ran out of time. I had to go and see Grandma Alice in the afternoon, and then there was all my homework to do."

"But why couldn't you have left it till Sunday? I can't believe you'd choose to stay at home and work when you could have been out with Saul. Anyway, we didn't have *that* much homework." Grace frowned. "You're not turning into some kind of swot, are you? Just because of what happened at the start of term? That was all Kelly's fault, remember? Not yours."

"Of course I'm not turning into a swot!" retorted Xanthe. "Swots are *brainy*, in case you hadn't noticed. The homework just took me a long time, that's all."

She flushed and glanced away. She hated lying to Grace. It was the worst thing about all this secrecy nonsense, but if she breathed a word to anyone outside the witching world she knew she would lose her powers. She smiled to herself – how did she suppose her friend would react if she *could* tell her the truth? *Oh, by the way, I thought you might as well know that I'm actually a witch. A True Witch, to be precise. That's why I've got that weird X-shaped birthmark on the back of my neck. Glowing Xs sometimes appear before my eyes, and if I concentrate on them hard enough I can reverse the evil deeds of Hexing Witches.* Grace would think she'd gone completely mad.

A wolf-whistle from the other side of the playground jolted her from her thoughts. A group of boys was standing with Saul, nudging him and pointing in her direction.

"I wish they'd cut it out," muttered Xanthe.

"Ignore them," said Grace. "They're only winding you up. Have you heard from him this weekend? He was definitely pining for you at the cinema."

"I might have done."

Grace rounded on her. "Oh, Xanthe! You should've told me! Has he asked you out?"

"Not exactly," replied Xanthe. "But he did send me a text asking if I wanted to meet up after school this week."

"*Result!*" exclaimed Grace. "I need details! When and where?"

"Tomorrow. I don't know where we're meeting

or anything, though."

"Well, he'll ask you out properly then, for sure. I *knew* it wouldn't be long."

Xanthe shrugged. "Maybe," she said. "I guess we'll just have to wait and see." She nudged Grace. "Anyway, what about *you*? Did Chris say anything to you on Saturday? Did he sit next to you at the cinema?"

Grace shook her head. "No, he didn't even come. Maybe he's not interested after all."

"But he talked to you at the party. He talked to you a *lot*."

"That doesn't necessarily mean he wants to go out with me. Now, leave it, will you? He's just walking in."

Xanthe's eyes drifted over to where a tall, dark-haired boy was heading towards the school gates. Not far behind him was Donna, her mobile pressed to her ear. Even from here, Xanthe could see the brightness in her eyes. Her face had the same rapt expression it had worn last Friday, when Xanthe had spotted her in the lunch queue.

As she approached the gates, Donna glanced up and caught Xanthe's eye, then frowned and bent her head.

Xanthe forced herself to look away. There was no doubt about it. That girl was up to something.

Miss Ambrose swept into the classroom in a voluminous ankle-length orange and purple dress.

"I promised you an interesting lesson today," she said, setting down a box of books and smiling round at the class. "And I don't think I'm going to disappoint you."

From her seat next to Grace, Xanthe smiled back. She liked English, and she liked Miss Ambrose, too. She was as colourful as her collection of dresses, and she had a way of making her lessons come alive.

"This term you get your first opportunity to study a couple of plays," her English teacher went on. "And we're going to start with one by the greatest playwright of all – William Shakespeare." She opened the box and began taking out the books and piling them on the desk. "What better way to introduce him to you than through one of his most famous tragedies – *Macbeth*."

A murmur went around the classroom. Alex Macpherson, Saul's best mate, tilted back his head and drew one finger across his throat.

"Ah," said Miss Ambrose. "I see you know a little about it then, Alex."

Alex shrugged. "Not really, Miss. Just that there's loads of fighting and blood and stuff."

Miss Ambrose grinned. "There is indeed. It's certainly one of the Bard's darkest plays." She came round to the front of her desk and leaned against it. "Does anyone know anything else about it? Can you name a few of the characters? Apart from Macbeth, of course."

Tilly Wilson put up her hand. "There's his wife, Miss. Lady Macbeth. Isn't she the crazy one who wanders around thinking she's got blood on her hands?"

Miss Ambrose laughed. "That's right, Tilly," she said. "And then there's Duncan and Banquo and Macduff and a whole raft of others. We'll get on to them later in the week. But what I want to concentrate on over the next few days is the general mood of the play. The *atmosphere*." She stood up and began handing out the books. "Who knows how it starts?"

The class looked blankly back at her.

"No one?" said Miss Ambrose. "Then I suggest we find out. Turn to Act 1, Scene 1, will you?"

Xanthe flicked through to the beginning of the play.

"*A desolate place*," she read. "*Thunder and lightning. Enter three witches*." Her mouth went dry. Oh, this was just great, wasn't it? An English lesson about witches. And with Donna sitting only three tables along from her, too. Whatever else she did, she mustn't catch her eye.

Miss Ambrose went back to the desk and perched on top of it.

"As you can see, Shakespeare uses a trio of witches to set the mood of the play," she explained. "They're also known as the Weird Sisters. In Shakespearian times, people very much believed in witches."

Some of the class started to snigger.

"Seriously, Miss?" asked Saul.

Miss Ambrose nodded. "Oh yes," she said. "It might seem ridiculous to us now, but back then women suspected of being witches were put to death."

Xanthe shuddered.

"What did they do to them?" asked Alex, leaning forward in his seat.

"Most often they would burn them," said Miss Ambrose. "They would put them through a trial by water first, tying them to ducking-stools and lowering them into a pond or river. If they floated, this was seen as proof they were witches. If they drowned they were innocent."

Alex's eyes widened. "That's gross."

Miss Ambrose nodded. "It is," she agreed. "Especially when you consider that most of the time these women had done nothing wrong. They were probably just outsiders. People who didn't fit into society." She smoothed down her dress. "Anyway, people also believed that witches could predict the future. And in just a very few lines Shakespeare uses the Weird Sisters to foretell Macbeth's fate. Let's get on and read it, shall we? Then you'll see what I mean. Do I have any volunteers? Does anyone fancy being a witch for the morning?"

Xanthe glared down at the table, wishing her powers stretched to becoming invisible. From the silence it was clear no one wanted to play the part of a witch.

"Very well," said Miss Ambrose. "I shall have to choose people myself." She scanned the room. "Grace and Xanthe, you can read First and Second Witches please, and Donna, you have a go at Third Witch. I'm sure you'll make an excellent trio."

Xanthe's heart plummeted. Just her luck to have been picked – and with Donna, too. From the other side of the classroom she could see Kelly sniggering into her textbook.

"When you're ready, then, girls. Really go to town with it. See if you can make your voices nice and witchy."

Xanthe bristled as the rest of the class laughed. *Nice and witchy*. What was that supposed to mean? Where had people ever got the idea that witches spoke in silly voices?

She sighed to herself. Who was she to talk? Two weeks ago she'd probably have laughed along with the rest of them. When Grandma Alice had first told her she was a True Witch, she'd scoured her great-grandmother's kitchen for evidence of magic. She'd expected to see a broomstick in the corner at the very least. But there'd been nothing. Not even the slightest hint.

"*When shall we three meet again?*" started Grace, her voice high and wheedling. "*In thunder, lightning, or in rain?*"

Xanthe cleared her throat. There was absolutely no way she was going to put on a stupid voice like that. She just wouldn't do it.

"*When the hurlyburly's done,*" she answered in deadpan tones. "*When the battle's lost and won.*"

"Hurlyburly means fighting or struggle, by the way," put in Miss Ambrose. "Shakespeare is using the witches to forecast the battle that is to come. Some would also argue they are predicting the battle for Macbeth's soul, but we won't worry too much about that right now. Carry on, please."

Silence fell around the room.

"Donna?" said Miss Ambrose, after another moment had passed. "Your turn."

"*That will be 'ere the set of sun,*" mumbled Donna, flushing.

Grace screwed her eyes up at Donna and Xanthe. She pulled out her ponytail and shook back her mane of black hair. "*Where the place?*" she screeched, half-rising to her feet.

Xanthe didn't look up from her book. How much worse could things get? Grace was actually *enjoying* this.

"*Upon the heath,*" she murmured.

"*There to meet with Macbeth,*" supplied Donna, so quietly that the rest of the class could scarcely hear her.

"Very good!" exclaimed Miss Ambrose. "Especially you, Grace. See if you can follow her example, Xanthe and Donna. Get into character a bit more. Maybe next week we'll go into the drama studio and dig out some costumes. Act a few scenes out properly." She turned back to Grace. "Right then, off you go again."

"*I come, Greymalkin!*" cried Grace.

Xanthe took a deep breath and scanned the next line. She hadn't the faintest clue what it meant.

"*Paddock calls,*" she murmured.

"Those two lines are references to spirits in animal shape," said Miss Ambrose, as if reading her mind. "I suppose you might call them witches' pets. Greymalkin is a cat and a paddock is a toad or a frog. They were given to a witch by Satan to help her with her sorcery and summon her to meetings.

And, Donna, your next line, '*Anon!*' just means, 'We're coming!' I know it all sounds a bit strange and old-fashioned, but you'll soon get used to it." She beamed. "Now, the last part all together, please."

Grace turned round and winked at Donna, who looked away at once. Xanthe kept her eyes glued to the book.

"*Fair is foul*," they intoned together, Grace's voice rising above the others', "*and foul is fair. Hover through the fog and filthy air.*"

Miss Ambrose clapped her hands. "Well done!" she cried. "An excellent start. I thought you did especially well, Grace. Very realistic. If I close my eyes I can just see you as an ugly old crone with straggly hair and a crooked nose."

Xanthe thought at once of Grandma Alice in her smart twin-sets and with her tidy hair, and stifled a giggle.

"Right then!" exclaimed Miss Ambrose. "We'll read it all through again, shall we? From the top, please, girls! And this time I promise I won't interrupt."

"What was the matter with you in there?" said Grace, as they filed out of the classroom at break. "You didn't get into the spirit of it at all. I thought you liked acting things out."

Xanthe shrugged. "I do usually," she said. "I guess I didn't think much of the play."

"And Donna was just as bad," Grace went on, ignoring her. "Mumbling away into her copy like she was reading nothing more interesting than the back of a cereal packet." She frowned. "Actually I was thinking about you two over the weekend. You didn't say a word to each other all last week. You haven't fallen out, have you?"

"Course not."

"Are you sure? You were getting on OK at the beginning of term, but now you seem to be going out of your way to avoid her."

"There's nothing wrong," insisted Xanthe. "She's – well, she's not my kind of person, that's all."

"She seems all right," replied Grace. "Not that she spoke much to me last week, either." She glanced up the corridor to where Donna was walking behind Saul. "Hang on a minute. You're not worried she's trying to steal Saul off you, are you? Just because they talk to each other sometimes doesn't mean there's anything going on between them."

"Of course I don't think that."

"Good," said Grace. "I'm glad to hear it." She sighed. "And whatever's got into you this morning, I wish you'd deal with it." She squeezed Xanthe's arm. "You've got no reason to be moody. All the trouble from the beginning of term is sorted, you've had the best thirteenth birthday party ever and the boy you fancy is about to ask you out. What more could you want? I mean…"

She broke off. Saul had dropped back from the crowd in front and was waiting for them to catch up with him.

"I'll – er – leave you to it," murmured Grace, as they drew alongside him. She scurried off after the rest of the class before Xanthe could protest.

For a moment neither of them spoke.

"Good weekend?" they blurted out at last in unison. They looked at one another and laughed.

"All right, I suppose," said Xanthe. "Bit boring. What about you? I take it you went out shopping for a new mobile?"

Saul nodded. "Dad treated me. He knew how gutted I was at losing the old one, and I kept telling him how it wasn't my fault. In any case, I need a phone for emergencies. It's not great, but it'll do for now. I'm still hoping the other one might turn up somewhere. I just can't work out how it went missing."

There was a short silence.

"Still OK for tomorrow?" he went on, staring at the ground.

Xanthe blushed and nodded. "Where d'you want to meet?"

"How about outside the newsagent's on the High Street?" suggested Saul. "Then I thought we could go down to the park."

Xanthe's heart sank. Of all the places to go on what might turn out to be her first ever date, she could think of a thousand better places than the scene of her recent battle with Donna.

"We could go somewhere else if you'd prefer," said Saul, glancing at her anxiously.

"No – no, the park's fine," said Xanthe, lowering her voice. They were nearly at the end of the corridor and Alex was waiting at the double doors, grinning at them. "I'll see you outside the newsagent's. About twenty to four?"

"Cool," murmured Saul. "See you then."

3.
The News

"It was a complete nightmare," said Xanthe, leaning back in her great-grandmother's rose-patterned armchair. "Worse than you can possibly imagine. And it's not going to get any better, either. Miss Ambrose wants us to spend the whole term acting bits out. We're probably going to go into the drama studio and dress up in some of the costumes."

Grandma Alice rolled her eyes. "Which will doubtless include long black cloaks and pointy hats," she said. She poured out two cups of tea and handed one to Xanthe. "Poor you. It must have been so irritating. If only they knew what we witches are *really* like."

"Well, they don't know," replied Xanthe. "And they never will." She sipped her tea. "Still, at least art was fun this afternoon. Miss Evans seems to have forgiven me for what happened the other week. She was lovely about the charcoal drawing I did as part of our project. Said it was one of the best pieces of work I've ever done." Her lips twitched. "She was really snappy with Kelly, though. It made me wonder if she now blames her for what happened with the paint."

Her great-grandmother sniffed.

"Good," she said. "That girl could do with being taken down a peg or two. I reckon Donna's done you a bit of a favour there, sweetheart."

Xanthe grinned. "So what about your day? Did you manage to get in touch with your True Witch contact? Peggy, isn't it? Weren't you hoping to tell her what happened between me and Donna?"

"I can't find her number. It must have been in that old address book I lost. Besides, it's probably out of date. I haven't been in touch with her for a good few years, and she's forever moving about the country. Never could settle down in one place."

"Isn't it possible she's not even a True Witch any more? She might have passed on the legacy by now. Like you did to me."

Grandma Alice shook her head. "She never had any children. Never even got married. Peggy'll be a practising True Witch until the day she dies." She sighed. "Oh, I do wish I'd made more of an effort to keep in contact with some of the others. I never really saw the point before, but at a time like this it would have been very useful." She reached down and stroked Blanche, who had sidled up beside her and was purring loudly. "Tell me, how's Donna been today? Apart from doing an even worse job of playing one of Shakespeare's witches than you, that is."

Xanthe shrugged. "Same as she was at the end of last week," she said. "She was talking to someone on her mobile again this morning before school. I'm convinced she's plotting something."

"It wouldn't surprise me. I just wish we knew whether or not she's said anything to her ancestor about what happened. Because if she has, half the Hexing Witch world will probably know by now. Rumour has it they're a far closer-knit bunch than us True Witches."

"But Grandma, we've been through all this before. If that were the case they'd already be after me. They'd have set up camp in Milchester and be watching my every move. And if they were that close, I'd be picking up their hexes, which I'm definitely *not* doing."

"I can't argue with your logic," replied her great-grandmother. "All the same, I'd be a lot happier if I could get hold of Peggy. I reckon there's a good chance she might be in touch with some of the other True Witches, and if I knew we had a bit of backing behind us, I'd relax a little. Don't forget it's been centuries since a True Witch and a Hexing Witch came into contact. I can't help worrying what the fall-out might be." She leaned forward and patted Xanthe's knee. "Plus of course I'm desperate to crow about what an amazing great-granddaughter I have. If I don't tell someone soon, I'll burst!"

Xanthe grunted. "I don't feel very amazing," she said. "Honestly, Grandma, I've been practising my concentration skills every spare second, and I still haven't picked anything up. I even locked myself in the toilets at lunchtime and tried then."

Her great-grandmother tutted. "How many times have I told you? It's still too early for you to be picking up hexes sparked from a long way off. You're going to have to wait. Honestly! I don't think I've ever known such impatience."

"But what if I've lost the knack?"

"*Lost the knack? You?* The girl who single-handedly defeated a Hexing Witch only days after her thirteenth birthday? The girl who conjured fire, like Ethelfreda did? I don't think so!"

Xanthe blushed. "But what if it was just a one-off?" she said. "What if…"

"What if, what if!" exclaimed Grandma Alice.

"I told you before, it doesn't work like that. You're a True Witch. You were born to reverse hexes. It's just a question of time, that's all. That, and a sensible amount of concentration practice."

"But I want to see them *now*."

Her great-grandmother winked at her. "And this from the girl who not so long ago wasn't even sure she *liked* the news that she was a True Witch. You're trying to run before you can walk, Xanthe. Be patient." She poured herself another cup of tea. "Did you manage to get all your homework done at the weekend?"

Xanthe pulled a face. "Not exactly. I spent so much time on my practice, I didn't get round to finishing my maths. I tried to do it on the bus to school and nearly missed my stop."

"Well, *that* won't do," said Grandma Alice. "You're going to have to manage your time a lot better than that." She frowned. "Are you telling me you spent the whole of Saturday evening staring at your bedroom wall when you could have been going out with your friends?"

Xanthe looked down into her teacup and said nothing.

"Once you start picking up hexes," her great-grandmother remarked gently, "things will never be the same again. Life will be one enormous juggle.

35

The only time you'll get a break will be when you shut your eyes at night. So make the most of this last bit of peace and quiet, and enjoy yourself. You probably won't have it again until you're my age."

Xanthe sighed. "I suppose I could do with lightening up." She blushed. "I'm meeting Saul after school tomorrow. I expect that'll take my mind off hexes for a while."

Grandma Alice smiled. "I expect it will," she said. "I look forward to hearing all about it." She glanced at the cuckoo clock and pulled herself to her feet. "But now I'm going to be very bossy and send you back home. You need to get on with your homework. In any case, it's nearly time for that new soap on TV. I can't wait to find out what's going to happen in the next episode."

Xanthe stood up and reached for her school bag. "You're turning into a right old telly addict," she teased. "All those years of using the TV as a cover while you were reversing hexes, and now you can't get enough of it."

Her great-grandmother laughed. "Call it my retirement present to myself. It's been a very long time coming."

She followed Xanthe down the corridor towards the front door.

"And I won't forget about Peggy, I promise.

I'll keep racking my brains about how to get in touch with her and I'll text you right away if I come up with anything."

Xanthe stooped to kiss her. "Thanks," she said, opening the door and stepping outside into the gathering dusk. "It'd be good to know there was someone on our side."

Xanthe stretched out on the sofa and picked up the remote.

For the first time in ages, it felt like she was actually back in control of her life. She'd taken Grandma Alice's advice to heart and decided against any concentration practice tonight, which meant that she'd finished all her homework – even the bits that weren't due in till the end of the week – and everything was packed away neatly inside her bag. Now, with Dad working upstairs and Mum chatting on the phone in the other room, she could chill out in front of one of her favourite programmes before bed.

She flicked on the TV, then frowned. Instead of the programme she'd been expecting, an unscheduled news bulletin was being broadcast: a young reporter was standing by the Thames, talking earnestly into a microphone.

"Despite a marked improvement in the weather,

the capital is continuing to experience rising water levels. For the first time in years, the Thames Barrier has been raised, though it's thought even this might not be enough to prevent the banks of the river from bursting."

Xanthe yawned. The news was always so boring. In any case, she could hardly keep her eyes open. She pulled a rug over her and snuggled deeper into the sofa. It wasn't surprising she was tired. Since discovering the truth about her inheritance, she'd stayed up late almost every night, either practising her concentration skills or writing in her diary. Even when she had eventually crawled into bed, her brain had often been buzzing too much for her to sleep. Grandma Alice was right. After the events of the last couple of weeks, she could definitely do with a rest.

Her thoughts turned to the following day and her heart lurched. She could hardly believe that this time tomorrow she and Saul would have been on their walk. *Was* he planning to ask her out, or had she got her wires crossed? What if he was fed up with all the teasing at school and just wanted to be friends after all?

She peered more closely at the screen as a series of aerial shots flashed up in front of her. It looked like things were really bad in London. The river was one vast churning whirlpool, and in the background the constant wail of sirens could be heard. She'd only been there twice – both times with Mum and Dad – but she still recognized quite a few of the buildings: Tower Bridge and the Gherkin, the Houses of Parliament and Big Ben. Oh, and there was the London Eye! She'd never been on that. Perhaps she could persuade her parents to take her and Grace at half-term. That would be so cool.

Picking up the remote again, she began flicking through the other channels, but almost all of them were covering the developing story in London.

She pulled back the rug and got off the sofa.

It didn't look like her programme was about to come on any time soon. She might as well go upstairs and get an early night.

4.
Hex

"Good news!" announced Miss Ambrose. "I've had a word with Mrs Jacobs in the drama studio and we thought it might be fun if you acted out a few scenes from *Macbeth* on stage later in the term. Possibly in front of an audience."

Xanthe groaned to herself.

"Soon we'll start looking at some of the main characters in the play and choose several of their big moments. But today I want to go back to the witches and read through another of their scenes. Turn to Act 4, Scene 1 in your copies, please."

Everyone leafed through the pages of their texts.

"Grace, I'd like to keep you as First Witch. The part clearly suits you. But Xanthe and Donna, if you don't mind I'm going to experiment with one or two of the others for Second and Third Witch. I didn't really feel either of you quite *connected* with the roles."

Xanthe felt herself go weak with relief. She settled back in her seat and grinned across at Grace. Out of the corner of her eye she could see Donna's pale face relax.

"Emma and Sarah – would you like to have a go?" asked Miss Ambrose. "Come up here to the whiteboard and we'll see if we can put in a few actions this time."

Xanthe watched as Grace and the others made their way to the front, clutching their copies.

Grace hunched her shoulders and beckoned Emma and Sarah close. "*Thrice the brindled cat hath mewed,*" she wheedled in her best witchy voice.

Emma gave her a toothy grin. "*Thrice and once the hedge-pig whined.*"

"What's a hedge-pig?" someone called out from the back.

"A hedgehog," replied Miss Ambrose. "Calling someone a hedge-pig in Shakespearian times was an insult."

"*Harpier cries, ''Tis time, 'Tis time,'*" screeched Sarah.

"A harpier is the Third Witch's pet," explained Miss Ambrose. "It's believed to be some sort of monstrous bird." She beamed at the trio of witches.

"Excellent, girls. I think we might have found the perfect combination. Now, Grace. Your turn again!"

Grace thrust out one hand and made a swirling motion in front of her.

"*Round about the cauldron go,*" she cackled. "*In the poisoned entrails throw…*"

Xanthe gazed into the distance. She tried to imagine Grandma Alice chucking bits of dead animal into a bubbling cauldron – and failed completely. Her great-grandmother's cooking skills had always been fairly basic: the best she usually managed to rustle up was a toasted sandwich or a boiled egg.

Grace had got to the end of her bit and now all three of them had their hands outstretched above the imaginary cauldron.

"*Double, double toil and trouble,*" they chorused together. "*Fire burn, and cauldron bubble.*"

The next moment Xanthe was jumping out of her seat.

"Xanthe!" Miss Ambrose hurried across the classroom towards her. "Whatever's the matter? Are you all right?"

Xanthe clutched the side of the table. In the centre of her vision was a huge glowing red X.

She blinked hard, trying to blot out the enormous shape that was pulsating in front of her. "It's OK. I've just got something in my eye, that's all."

"Do you want to go and bathe it in some water?"

"Yes, please," mumbled Xanthe. "I-I won't be long." She stumbled out of the classroom, her head bent. She could sense everyone was looking at her, and it wasn't difficult to imagine who was staring the hardest. The last thing she wanted to do right now was catch Donna's eye.

Closing the door behind her, she made straight for the nearest girls' cloakroom and stood beside one of the basins, gripping the taps. The X had faded now, though the shape was still imprinted on her brain.

She let out a long, slow breath. She'd seen one. She'd actually seen one. And just when she'd given up hope, too.

But why had she seen it so soon? Was it because she'd put in all those hours of practice, or was there another reason? The hex hadn't been Donna's doing, she was pretty sure of that: nothing terrible had happened to her, as it had done at the start of term, when her maths test had been scrawled over, or when her experiment had exploded in science.

No – this hex hadn't been *aimed* at her. She had simply picked it up because the person sparking it was close by: some of the other Hexing Witches must have heard about her battle with Donna and decided to come to Milchester to get their revenge. They were closing in on her.

She shivered.

One thing made no sense. When the X had flashed up in front of her, she hadn't been concentrating. All those hours of staring at her bedroom wall, and when the moment had finally arrived she'd been in a sort of daydream, half listening to what was going on around her and half thinking about something else. It wasn't at all as Grandma Alice had predicted.

And why had it been so big? The glowing Xs she had seen before hadn't been half that size. She'd been so shocked by its appearance that she hadn't even thought to look at its surroundings, let alone attempt to reverse it.

Xanthe sighed. It seemed like there were an awful lot of unanswered questions, and the only person who could help her solve them was Grandma Alice. The moment the bell rang for lunch, she would find a quiet corner and phone her.

For now, though, she needed to get back to English. Miss Ambrose would be wondering where she was. She turned on the tap and splashed water over her face. At least she'd better *look* like she'd been bathing her eye.

Straightening up, she glanced at her reflection in the mirror and felt a small stab of pride. She might not have been Miss Ambrose's idea of a Shakespearian witch, but what did it matter when she was the real thing?

"Are you sure you're OK?" asked Grace. "You scared the life out of me, jumping up from the table like that. It was as if you'd had some sort of vision."

Xanthe followed her up the stairs towards the lockers. "I told you. I'm fine. I just got something in my eye."

"It looks all right to me," said Grace. "It's not even red or anything." At the top of the stairs she turned to face her friend. "You haven't seen another of those glowing shapes, have you? You know, like the ones you were telling me about at the beginning of term?"

Xanthe flushed crimson. "Of course I haven't!" she muttered. "And keep your voice down, will you? I don't want the whole class thinking I'm off my head." She put her books in her locker. "I'll see you in the canteen in a few minutes. I need to give Grandma Alice a quick call. She's – well, she's a bit fragile at the moment and I promised I'd check up on her. Bag me a place in the lunch queue, will you? I won't be long."

She watched as Grace shut her locker and disappeared back down the stairs. Perhaps she'd be better off texting her great-grandmother, rather than phoning her. It was never easy finding anywhere properly private at lunchtime. The playground was always heaving with students, and the girls' cloakrooms were full of people doing their hair and trying on make-up. A bit of quiet texting in the library would be a much safer bet.

Donna was lingering just outside the library, and shot her a sly grin as she went past. Xanthe looked away at once. It wasn't hard to imagine what was on *her* mind right now. She clearly knew all too well what had happened in English.

Apart from a few sixth formers slogging away in the special study area, the library was practically empty. Xanthe sat down at a table in the corner and let the morning's events sink in. The more she thought about it, the more she reckoned Donna must have swallowed her pride and told her ancestor what had happened between them. Why else would she have seen that X? There had to be Hexing Witches in Milchester, surely? She wouldn't have had the power to pick up a hex sparked from any further away.

Shuddering, she huddled over her mobile and keyed in a text to Grandma Alice. *Have picked up a hex*, she wrote. *Feeling a bit scared.*

Her mobile beeped with a message almost at once. *You can't have*, her great-grandmother had replied. *You must have been imagining things!*

Xanthe pursed her lips. What did Grandma Alice take her for?

I wasn't imagining anything, she texted back. *I saw a glowing X.*

There was a pause before her great-grandmother replied. *Did anything bad happen? Like it did before?*

No. Nothing happened. Donna was there in the room but I don't think it was sparked by her.

Grandma Alice responded straight away. *Don't like the sound of this AT ALL. Come and see me directly after school.*

Xanthe frowned. Grandma Alice had obviously forgotten what she was doing this afternoon. *Can't come then. I'm meeting Saul, remember?*

Well, you'll have to cancel. You can't go wandering around Milchester with THIS going on. It's not SAFE.

Xanthe's mouth went dry. She hadn't thought of that. She'd been so caught up wondering what Saul might be planning to say to her this afternoon, it hadn't even crossed her mind that their walk might turn out to be dangerous.

Her hands shook slightly as she keyed in her next message. *But, Grandma, what shall I do? If I don't turn up, he'll think I don't like him.*

You'll have to think of an excuse. This is serious, Xanthe. Come straight round after school. And BE CAREFUL.

Xanthe sat back in her chair. She'd never known

47

Grandma Alice to be so stern before. There was no point arguing with her – and anyway, she was talking perfect sense. It would be madness to wander round an exposed place like the park when in all likelihood there were Hexing Witches in Milchester. But what was she going to do about Saul? What was she going to *say* to him?

She started as a familiar figure approached and sat down at a nearby table. It was Donna.

Xanthe watched as she took an encyclopedia from the bookshelf and propped it up in front of her. She pursed her lips. It looked like Donna was about to do a little secret texting of her own.

Moments later she heard her whispering into her mobile. Xanthe's eyes widened. She was taking a bit of a risk, wasn't she? The librarian usually ignored texting, but if she caught anyone making an actual phone call she'd give them a detention on the spot. And why had Donna chosen to sit so close to her? She must have seen her, surely? It was almost as if she was doing it deliberately.

"Just let me know as soon as you can," she heard Donna mutter. "And of *course* I want to be part of the plan."

Xanthe swallowed. What was that supposed to mean? Part of what plan? Something aimed at her? Something cooked up by the Hexing Witches to get their revenge?

"And it doesn't matter if you need to call during school hours," Donna murmured. "Just send me a text and I'll find a quiet place to ring you back. I'll have my phone with me all the time."

She rang off and pushed the encyclopedia roughly to one side, then marched out of the library without a backwards glance.

Xanthe stared after her, her heart pounding.

Things were getting more and more worrying.

5.
The Warning

Xanthe checked her watch.

In five minutes she should have been meeting Saul outside the newsagent's and heading for the park. Perhaps they would have stopped at the café beside the swings and bought a drink before going on to look at the burned-out shell of the boathouse. By the time they reached the lake he might even have asked her out. Instead of which she was walking up the path towards Grandma Alice's front door, her heart heavier than she had ever known it.

She'd managed to put a brave face on things at lunch, but once afternoon school had begun and she was alone with her thoughts again, the problem of what she was going to say to Saul had come rushing back and she'd found it impossible to concentrate.

She hadn't had a clue what to say to Grace, either. Luckily at the end of their last lesson her friend had been up at the front of the classroom going through something she didn't understand with the teacher, so as soon as the bell had rung Xanthe had just bolted out of school, not even bothering to go to the lockers to sort out her books. The last thing she'd wanted was to be spotted, so she'd sprinted straight past the bus stop, checking over her shoulder now and again for anyone suspicious-looking who might be following her, and run halfway to Grandma Alice's house before stopping to text Saul.

Really sorry, but my great-grandmother's ill, she'd lied. *Mum needs someone to sit with her till she gets back from work. Can you make another day?*

Then she'd switched off her mobile to avoid either him or Grace phoning to ask any difficult questions. Not that Saul was likely to reply. He'd probably be way too mad at her.

She rang Grandma Alice's doorbell and waited.

"What a relief to see you!" said her great-grandmother, appearing at the door almost at once. "Come along through, sweetheart."

Xanthe gave her a hug and followed her into the sitting room.

"What did you tell Saul?" asked Grandma Alice, as they sat down opposite one another.

"I told him you were ill and needed looking after," said Xanthe, staring down at her hands. "It was the best I could come up with."

Grandma Alice sighed. "I'm really sorry to mess up your plans. But you must see we needed to talk urgently. And I didn't want you hanging around Milchester – it would have been far too risky."

"You reckon there must be Hexing Witches nearby, don't you? You think they must have found out about me and Donna, and come to Milchester to get their own back?"

"I don't know what to think. But yes, it's a possibility. I certainly don't want you wandering around town until we work out what's going on. And I don't want you anywhere *near* the park. If there are Hexing Witches in Milchester, they'll be nosing around down there for sure. They'll want to see for themselves where it all took place." She stood up. "Look, I'll get us both a drink and then you can tell me exactly what happened today."

Xanthe watched as her great-grandmother disappeared into the kitchen, then she slid her hand into her pocket and switched on her mobile.

There were no messages from Saul, but Grace had left her one, and she sounded pretty hacked off.

Why did you rush off like that? I wanted to say good luck.

Xanthe sighed. What was it Grandma Alice had

said to her yesterday? *Once you start picking up hexes, things will never be the same again.* Well, that was turning out to be true enough. And sooner than she'd thought, too. She put her mobile back in her pocket. Perhaps Saul would text her later on. Perhaps he'd be OK about it after all and give her another chance.

Her great-grandmother came back into the sitting room, carrying a tray. Blanche trotted in behind her and jumped on to Xanthe's lap.

"So go on then," said Grandma Alice, when they were sipping their hot chocolates. "Tell me about the moment you picked up the hex. I want to know every last detail."

Xanthe shrugged.

"There's not much to tell," she said. "Except to say that I wasn't actually concentrating when it happened."

"You weren't *concentrating*?"

"No, I was kind of staring into space, half listening to the others reading out their scene from *Macbeth*, and suddenly there it was: this massive great glowing X. It was enormous – much bigger than the ones I saw the last two times."

Grandma Alice frowned. "How very odd," she said. "In my experience, the Xs don't usually vary much in size. And goodness knows how you managed to pick one up when you weren't even concentrating." She took another sip of hot chocolate. "What about the surroundings to the hex? Could you make anything out?"

"I didn't notice. It was stupid of me, I know. And I didn't try to reverse it, either. I was standing there in the middle of the classroom with everyone staring at me, and all I wanted was for it to go away."

"I don't blame you. It's a wonder you managed to keep your head at all."

Xanthe stroked Blanche's sleek white fur. "So what d'you reckon's going on?"

Her great-grandmother leaned back in her armchair. "I don't know," she replied. "I really don't. The way you describe it, it's as if the hex you picked up had a special sort of strength to it. A *new* sort of strength." She wrung her hands. "Oh, I *wish* I could get hold of Peggy. She'd know what to do. She always had a calm head on her shoulders."

Xanthe said nothing. It seemed they were in this on their own.

"I suppose for now we'll have to assume the worst," went on Grandma Alice. "That Donna has told her ancestor what happened and that there are Hexing Witches close by, hoping to get their revenge on you." She shivered and glanced out of the window. "Look, I know you've only just got here, but I think you should probably head home before it starts to get dark. Would you like me to ring your mother and ask her to come and collect you?"

Xanthe shook her head. "You can't wrap me up in cotton wool, Grandma. I've got to *live*. I agree it might be a good idea to avoid the park for a bit, but I can't just shut myself away at home, can I? I need to get to and from school for a start."

"You're right, of course," said Grandma Alice, getting to her feet. "But *please* be careful, and text me the moment you're back." She came forward and hugged Xanthe. "Let me know if you see another hex, won't you? And try not to worry about Saul. If he's worth anything he'll rearrange his date with you, I'm sure." She gave a rueful smile. "I lost count of the number of times I stood up my Bill because of some wretched hex or other, but he never gave up on me. I'm afraid life as a True Witch can be a right old juggle."

Xanthe tugged on her coat and reached for her bag. As far as she could work out, a right old juggle didn't come close.

Xanthe stood inside the hallway and breathed in deeply.

It was such a relief to be home. Mum was back

from work early and, judging by the delicious smell wafting from the kitchen, she was in the middle of one of her marathon baking sessions. The news was blaring from the radio: an update on the worsening crisis in London.

Xanthe smoothed down her hair. The walk back from Grandma Alice's had totally freaked her out. She'd half run the last part, glancing behind her every few seconds and starting at the slightest noise. She was nearly at the front gate when their next-door neighbour had scuttled out in front of her with a binbag of rubbish and she'd almost died of fright.

"Hi!" her mother called from the kitchen. "You're a bit late!"

Xanthe took off her coat and hung it on the peg behind the door. "Sorry! I dropped round to see Grandma Alice. I won't be a minute. I'm just going up to my room to change."

Halfway up the stairs her mobile rang. She fumbled in her pocket to answer it.

"Hello?"

"Xanthe, it's me," came back Grace's voice. "What on earth's going on? I've just seen Saul in town with some of his mates."

"Hang on a second." Xanthe ran up the remaining stairs and shut herself in her room, then sank down on her bed. "You – you didn't speak to him, did you?"

"Of course not. I wouldn't do that without ringing you first. Where are you?"

Xanthe cupped her hand round her mobile. "I'm at home. There's – well, there's been a problem."

"What sort of a problem?"

There was a moment's pause.

"Look, are you going to tell me what's happened, or not?" asked Grace. "I left you a message in case you hadn't noticed. Why didn't you wait for me at the end of school?"

Xanthe hesitated. She'd better stick to the same story she'd told Saul and hope Grace didn't mention anything to Mum or Dad. It was risky, but right now she couldn't think of a better plan. "I got a text from Mum saying Grandma Alice wasn't well. She – she needed someone to sit with her till she got back from work. I had to get there as soon as I could."

"You mean you didn't meet up with Saul at all?"

"Got it in one."

Grace's tone of voice changed at once. "Oh, *Xanthe*! That's such bad luck. Was he OK about it?"

"I don't know. I haven't spoken to him. I was in such a rush to get to Grandma Alice's, I only had time to send a text."

"And he hasn't replied?"

"Not yet."

"Well, I'm sure he'll get back to you soon," said

Grace. "How's Grandma Alice, anyway? It's nothing serious, I hope."

"Oh – er, no. She just had a bit of a dizzy spell, that's all. I expect she'll be fine after a good night's sleep." Xanthe stood up and walked over to the window. She suddenly felt very weary. "Look, I'd better go. I'm tired and fed up and I want to get changed. I'll see you tomorrow, OK?"

Ringing off, she rested her head against the window pane. What sort of a person was she turning into? Today she'd told lies to two of the most important people in her life. OK, so they weren't serious lies, not the type that were actually going to hurt anyone – but they were lies all the same.

She gazed out into the gloom of the evening, scanning the street for any signs of unusual activity. For all she knew, there might be a Hexing Witch watching her this very moment.

She drew the curtains and shuddered.

When it came down to it, a few white lies were probably the least of her worries.

6.
The Phone Call

Xanthe picked up her bag and followed Grace out of the science lab.

She was going to have to pluck up courage and say something to Saul. He still hadn't replied to her text, and had been avoiding her all morning, sitting at the opposite end of the room and looking away every time she glanced in his direction. He'd even teamed up with someone else when they were doing experiments, instead of being her lab partner as usual. It didn't take a genius to see he was mad at her.

She sighed to herself.

If only she'd had the guts to send him that second text last night. She'd worked out what to say and keyed it into her mobile – a short message saying how sorry she was and how bad she felt at letting him down – but she hadn't quite managed to press the send button. What if it made her come across as whiney and pathetic? Or worse still, too keen? It was complete torture – things had been so much easier between them before.

She leaned in towards Grace. "I'm going to catch Saul before he heads outside for break," she whispered. "I won't be long."

Grace nodded. "Good luck," she said. "I'll see you in a minute."

Xanthe hung back from the rest of the class and scoured the corridor. Saul was walking a short distance behind with Alex, frowning to himself and kicking his bag out in front of him.

Her heart lurched as she made her way towards him.

"Hi there," she murmured.

Alex winked at Saul. "Looks like your girlfriend wants to talk to you, mate."

Saul went bright red and elbowed his friend in the ribs. "Shut up, will you? Why don't you do us all a favour and get lost?"

Alex grinned and sauntered off after the others.

"Sorry about that," said Saul into the silence that followed.

Xanthe cleared her throat. "I–I just wanted to say sorry about yesterday. You – well, you must've thought I didn't want to come."

Saul stared down at the ground. "I didn't know what to think."

Xanthe forced herself to go on. "Look, Saul, I'm really close to my great-grandma. I always have been." She paused. That bit, at least, was true. "So when Mum texted me to say she wasn't well, and that she needed me to go and sit with her, I had to. You can ask Grace if you don't believe me."

"Of course I believe you. But why didn't you just come and tell me? Or at least *ring* me? All I got was a stupid text."

Xanthe flushed. "I'm sorry," she said, biting her lip. "Could we try again?"

Saul shrugged. He stopped at the foot of the stairs leading up to the lockers and fiddled with the strap on his bag. "Well, I've got band practice after school tonight, but I suppose I could do tomorrow." He managed a small smile. "Same plan as before?"

Xanthe smiled back at him. "Perfect. Though I'd rather give the park a miss, if that's all right. Mum and Dad aren't too keen on me going down there at the moment."

Saul nodded. "I should have thought of that before." He slung his bag over his shoulder. "I hope they catch whoever did it. They lost all the boats, you know, as well as the building. It means we probably won't be able to go out rowing till the autumn."

Xanthe said nothing. She just prayed she didn't look too guilty.

"Anyway," went on Saul. "I'm sure we can find something else to do. Go to a café in town, maybe."

"That'd be great," said Xanthe. "I'll see you after school tomorrow, then. And this time I promise I'll be there."

They grinned at each other and Xanthe watched as Saul hurried up the stairs after the rest of the class. She turned and made her way towards the playground. She'd go and put her books away in a minute, once everyone else had come down for break. She couldn't face appearing beside the lockers with Saul. She'd never hear the end of it.

Donna was standing by the double doors leading out into the playground, fiddling with her mobile. She looked up as Xanthe passed and raised her eyebrows.

Xanthe ignored her and walked into the playground, a warm glow spreading over her. She'd done it. She'd actually sorted things out so she had another chance with Saul. She'd *never* have been able to do that a few weeks ago. She wouldn't have had the guts.

Donna walked slowly past, her head bent over her phone. "All right, then," Xanthe heard her say.

"Sounds great to me. I'll speak to you later, when you've got more information. Yes, yes – whenever suits. Just text me, OK? I'll get out of lessons if I have to."

Xanthe swallowed. The warm glow she had felt only moments before had evaporated completely, and in its place was cold dread. There was no question that Donna was up to something – and she clearly wasn't acting alone, either.

She reached inside her skirt pocket and closed her fingers round the smooth casing of her locket. She simply *had* to find out what the Hexing Witches were planning – and with Grandma Alice no closer to getting hold of Peggy, it looked like she was going to have to do it by herself.

They were about ten minutes into afternoon lessons when she saw it: an X, bigger than the one she'd picked up yesterday and glowing with such intensity it made her eyes smart.

Xanthe bowed her head, hoping that Donna wouldn't glance over and suspect something was up. Miss Pimm was lost in a world of her own, droning on about their new maths topic, and it didn't look like she was about to stop any time soon. With luck she'd be able to examine this X properly.

It had appeared in much the same way as it had done in English. She'd been sitting back in her chair, thinking about what she'd overheard Donna saying in the playground at break and wondering for the hundredth time what it might mean, when the X had flashed up in front of her like a massive red beacon, sharp and clear and impossibly bright.

Focusing her attention away from the shape itself, she allowed her eyes to drift over its surroundings, but all she could make out was a vague, watery greyness.

Grace nudged her. "Are you OK?" she whispered.

Xanthe nodded, trying to ignore the interruption, but it was no good. Already her concentration was broken and the X was starting to fade.

A faint beeping noise a few tables to her right had her looking up. Someone must have switched their mobile on. She glanced round to see Donna fumbling inside her pocket, her face flushed. The next moment her hand was shooting up. "Miss Pimm?"

Miss Pimm broke off from her lecture and frowned. "Yes, Donna? What is it?"

"May I be excused?"

Miss Pimm sighed. "Yes, but hurry up. I don't want you missing out on anything important."

Xanthe waited until Donna had closed the door behind her, then put up her hand. This was her chance to find out what was going on. "I'm sorry, Miss Pimm, but I need to be excused, too."

Miss Pimm raised her eyebrows. "Honestly! You've just had lunchbreak. You should have gone then. Don't be long, please."

Xanthe made her way out of the classroom and crept towards the girls' cloakroom, looking out for Donna as she went. She had nearly reached the cloakroom when she heard a familiar voice coming from the side corridor leading to the drama studio.

"So they reckon they're getting close?" Donna was hissing into her phone. "They think it'll burst its banks sometime over the next few days?"

Xanthe frowned. What on earth was Donna talking about?

"You mean they need extra forces? *Tomorrow?* Well, yes, of course I'd love to be there, I told you before. But how can I? It's a school day."

There was a brief pause.

"Yes, yes, I can see how important it is. As many of us as possible. Look, I'll find a way, all right? I'll get back to you later on. I think there's a London train in the morning just after half eight. If I caught that and took the tube from Victoria, I could probably be down near the river for ten."

Xanthe pressed herself against the wall, hardly daring to breathe.

"OK, then. I'll speak to you this evening. Bye."

There was the sound of footsteps as Donna walked back up towards the main corridor. Xanthe dived into the cloakroom and shut herself in one of the cubicles, her pulse racing.

She stood there for a few moments, replaying Donna's words over and over in her head: *They're getting close … it'll burst its banks sometime over the next few days … they need extra forces … as many of us as possible … there's a London train in the morning just after half eight … I could probably be down near the river for ten."*

Her mind flicked back to the news bulletin she'd seen on TV the other evening – and then to the watery surroundings of the hex she had just picked up.

She shivered. These hexes weren't being sparked by witches closing in on Milchester, were they? They weren't connected to some nasty little personal vendetta aimed at her.

They were evidence of mischief on a much grander scale.

Xanthe sat at the back of the bus and willed it to go faster. If she didn't get things off her chest soon she reckoned she'd explode.

She could still hardly believe what she'd heard in the corridor. The knowledge that TV screens all over the country were flashing up images of a city threatened not by the power of nature, but by the evil deeds of Hexing Witches, was almost impossible to take in. Of course, it was a relief to know she wasn't in danger herself, but all the same ... this was far more serious troublemaking than her great-grandmother had ever suggested the witches were capable of.

It all made perfect sense, though: the way the Thames kept rising in spite of the improvement in the weather; the inability of the authorities to explain what was going on. And no wonder she'd started seeing Xs – by the sound of things, there were several Hexing Witches at work down there already; their combined forces were bound to spark hexes of unparalleled strength.

Xanthe frowned down at her mobile. Why wasn't Grandma Alice responding to her texts? She'd sent her one the moment she'd come out of maths, and then another as soon as the bell had rung at the end of school, but so far all she'd picked up in return was a message her great-grandmother had sent just after the start of afternoon lessons – around the time she'd been listening in on Donna's conversation. *Have had a brainwave*, it read. *Think I know how to get hold of*

Peggy. Will report back soon. GGA xx.

Xanthe ran her finger over her mobile. The message was some comfort, at least. It was good to know they might at last have some real support, especially now things were getting so serious. If her great-grandmother was right and Peggy was a calm, clear-thinking sort of person, then maybe she would come up with a plan. Perhaps she'd suggest following Donna to London. She might even be allowed to tag along herself.

She started as a familiar shape appeared before her eyes, surrounded by the same watery greyness she'd seen before. Another hex! And this time she wasn't in the middle of a lesson with her classmates. She might actually be able to *do* something about this one.

She filtered out the rumble of the bus and the chatter of the other passengers and focused every atom of her being on the X in front of her, but the more she concentrated the brighter it seemed to burn. In the end she was forced to look away, her eyes watering from the intensity of the glowing shape.

Her stop came into view and she hurried to the front of the bus.

At least now she knew what she was up against. At least she knew *why* these Xs were so big and strong.

And in a couple of minutes she'd be able to share the whole incredible story with Grandma Alice.

7.
The Note

Xanthe pressed her face against the kitchen window and peered inside.

Something wasn't right. She'd rung the bell three times and still there was no sign of Grandma Alice. Her great-grandmother never took this long to answer. What was more, Blanche had practically shot out of the cat flap when she had walked down the path a few minutes earlier and was now twisting herself round her legs, mewing loudly.

She went round the side of the house and hammered on the back door.

Where on earth was she? Grandma Alice hardly ever went out, and anyway, she was under strict instructions from the district nurse not to leave the house at the moment – not until her hip was completely better.

Xanthe took out her phone and dialled her great-grandmother's mobile. Immediately she was redirected to voicemail.

"Where are you?" she demanded into the silence. "I'm getting worried. Ring me back when you get this message. Loads to tell."

She picked up Blanche, who had followed her like a shadow, and rested her chin on the cat's soft white head. Was it possible this had something to do with the text about Peggy? Had her great-grandmother disobeyed the district nurse and headed into Milchester to get some information? Perhaps she'd gone to the library to use the computers. That didn't seem very likely, though – she was useless with modern technology.

She jumped as her phone began to ring.

"Xanthe, it's me," came her mother's voice, a little breathless. "I'm at the hospital."

"*The hospital?* What's happened?"

"It's Grandma Alice. She's had a fall. Quite a nasty one, I'm afraid."

Xanthe set Blanche down on the back doorstep, trying to quell the panic that was rising inside her. "Is she all right? Have you seen her?"

"Only very briefly," replied her mother. "I went straight to the hospital as soon as they called me at work, but they wouldn't let me stay longer than a few minutes. They're getting her ready to take down to the operating theatre."

"*What?*"

"Don't worry. She's going to be OK. They've done some X-rays and they're pretty sure she hasn't done herself any permanent damage. But it looks like she's fractured her dodgy hip, and possibly one of her arms, too. And of course she's bruised all over and very badly shaken."

Xanthe sank down beside Blanche and gathered her into her lap. "How did it happen?"

"I'm not completely sure. She won't say much about it. But the ambulance crew found her on the floor in the spare room surrounded by cardboard boxes full of letters, and we think she might have been climbing on a chair to get another box down from the shelf. Luckily she had her mobile to hand and managed to call for help. The ambulance crew got in through an open window."

"Can I go and see her?"

"Not today. She's not allowed visitors until tomorrow evening at the earliest. They said they'd let us know – and, of course, they'll update us as soon as she's had her operation."

Xanthe stumbled to her feet, still clutching Blanche. "But I've *got* to see her before then. There's – there's something I need to talk to her about."

"Well, I'm afraid whatever it is will just have to wait. The hospital made it quite clear no one's to bother her until at least tomorrow night."

"But, Mum…"

"Leave it, Xanthe. The answer's no." Her mother's voice softened. "Look, I'm on my way home now. Try not to fret. I'm sure she'll be fine."

Xanthe cradled Blanche closer.

"Oh, I nearly forgot," went on her mother. "Grandma Alice gave me a note for you."

"A *note*?"

"Yes. She was very secretive about it, too. Scribbled it on the back of an old envelope and folded it up about six times so I wouldn't see what it said. She insisted I pass it on the moment you got in from school."

Xanthe closed her eyes and buried her face in Blanche's fur.

Maybe her great-grandmother had managed to do a little amateur detective work after all.

"I've never seen anything like it!" exclaimed Mr Fox, gaping at the TV. "If the river bursts its banks, the entire city will be flooded. It'll be a full-scale national crisis."

Xanthe stared at the screen. It was true. The Thames looked like something out of one of those end-of-the-world action movies – the ones where mankind has to fight against some kind of supreme natural force in order to save the species. Except this wasn't a movie, and the London authorities weren't struggling against anything even remotely natural.

"*In spite of raising the Thames Barrier, the river is now close to breaking point,*" the reporter was saying. "*Every effort has been made to drain it, but water levels have not stopped rising, and the city has been placed on amber alert. People living near the Thames are being urged to protect their properties with sandbags. Bus and Underground networks are operating a restricted service, and trains into the capital are subject to delay and cancellation.*"

Mrs Fox frowned. "It's very odd, isn't it? I mean, *why* isn't the water draining away? It hasn't rained since the weekend – surely things should have eased by now? It doesn't make any sense."

Xanthe pursed her lips. To her it made perfect sense. The river wasn't churning with normal water. It was churning with hexed water – water that wouldn't drain away however much you tried to make it. Somewhere in London there was a gang of Hexing Witches hell-bent on causing more destruction to the capital than it had seen in centuries.

She felt for her great-grandmother's note in her pocket, recalling every word of it.

Contact Dulcie Miller. Old schoolfriend of Peggy's. She will have her number, it read. *Letter from her somewhere in box in spare room. Dulcie NOT TW, so BE CAREFUL.*

Xanthe sighed. Grandma Alice had obviously been searching for this letter from Dulcie and fallen trying to reach one of the boxes. If only she'd waited till later on – then they could have looked for it together.

Still, there was no point dwelling on what might have been. She had to face facts. Grandma Alice was stuck in hospital with a fractured hip and a total ban on visitors, and she was stuck at home with a nightmare on her hands and no one to discuss it with.

Xanthe blinked away another hex. She'd picked up three since supper, and each time they'd proved impossible to do anything about; she'd only managed to focus on the third one for a couple of seconds before she'd had to look away. It had been like looking at the sun on a bright summer's day.

She racked her brains. She needed to come up with a plan – and fast. With her great-grandmother out of the picture for at least the next twenty-four hours, the only person she could talk to about the situation was Peggy. She'd tried to persuade Mum that she ought to return to Grandma

Alice's house that evening to check on Blanche, but her mother had said there was no need to worry about her till the morning – she'd dropped in herself on her way back from the hospital to feed the cat and pick up her great-grandmother's mobile. Apparently Grandma Alice had made no end of fuss about leaving it behind and had practically begged for it to be brought in the following evening. She'd also made it clear that no one was even to *think* about accessing her messages.

Xanthe thought back to the wording of the note. *BE CAREFUL*, her great-grandmother had written, and it was easy to see what she meant. If Dulcie wasn't a True Witch – if she was just an ordinary friend of Peggy's – then she was going to have to watch what she said to her on the phone. There could be no mention of hexes or special powers or witches of either variety.

She stared up at the ceiling, trying to organize her thoughts. The first part of tomorrow would be fairly simple. She would go over to Grandma Alice's as early as possible, find the letter and, if luck was on her side, get hold of Peggy's number from Dulcie and ring her.

And then – well, then life was going to get a whole lot trickier.

Because whatever happened with Peggy – whether

she managed to speak to her or not – Xanthe knew what she had to do next.

Someone had to find out where the Hexing Witches were operating from.

And that meant following Donna to London.

8.
Peggy

Xanthe let herself into Grandma Alice's house and hurried through into the kitchen. Blanche followed, brushing against her legs. The little cat had been waiting on the doorstep when she'd arrived, and clearly wasn't going to let her out of her sight.

She glanced down at Blanche's food bowl. No need to top up that, then. The food Mum had left out yesterday hadn't even been touched.

"Poor thing," she murmured, bending to stroke the cat's head. "It doesn't feel right without her, does it?"

Dumping her bag on the floor, Xanthe picked up the phone and dialled the school office. She selected *Absences* from the main menu and waited until the automated voice at the other end of the line asked her to leave her details.

"Xanthe Fox," she mumbled into the phone, trying her best to sound like her mother. "Class 8C. I'm afraid Xanthe won't be in school today as she is unwell."

She placed the phone back in the receiver and took a small rucksack out of her bag. In it was a waterproof and a street map of London she'd found in one of the bookcases at home. With any luck she wouldn't need the map – she'd just have to follow Donna from the train into the Underground – but it'd be good to have it with her in case of emergency.

From the bottom of her bag she pulled out a hoodie and a pair of jeans – there was no way she was going to risk turning up at the station in Milchester High uniform. That would be sure to attract attention. Changing quickly, she transferred her locket from her skirt pocket to her jeans, stuffed her school clothes into her bag and hid it in one of the kitchen cupboards. Then she made for the spare room, still shadowed by Blanche.

The room was just as Mum had described it – strewn with letters and cardboard boxes. An upturned chair lay beneath a row of shelves, and on the top shelf sat two unopened boxes.

Xanthe looked at her watch. She had a few minutes to make a start on one of the boxes, but if she didn't find Dulcie's letter pretty much immediately she'd have to come back later and look for it then. She couldn't risk missing the train and losing Donna.

Righting the upturned chair, she climbed on top of it and reached for the nearest box.

She squatted down on the floor to open it. It was packed with bundles of letters and postcards, held together by rubber bands. By the looks of things, the whole of her great-grandmother's personal history was inside these boxes: thousands of words sent to her by friends and relatives, dating back years and years.

Xanthe began sorting through the bundles. Thank goodness Grandma Alice had always been so organized. Everything was neatly labelled: *Letters from schoolfriends; Postcards from friends; Letters from Bill.*

Her eyes drifted over the thick pile of letters from Great-granddad Bill – most likely love letters, sent before her great-grandparents were married. It didn't feel right, somehow, even looking at the faded envelopes. It was as if she was intruding into Grandma Alice's private life.

She placed the pile gently to one side. There was just enough time to go through a few of the bundles, and then she'd have to leg it to the station. She undid the rubber band from a stack labelled *Letters from friends* and began sifting through them, checking the bottom of each for a name.

And suddenly there it was: *with love from Dulcie*, looped across the page in flowery handwriting – and at the top of the letter, printed beside the address in the left-hand corner, the thing she'd been searching for.

The phone number that would surely lead her to Peggy.

Xanthe put on her rucksack and pulled up her hood to shield herself from anyone who might recognize her on the way to the station. Then she let herself out of the front door and walked down the path towards the gate.

She couldn't help smiling to herself. She'd rung Dulcie, who had answered straight away, and a couple of minutes later she'd been scribbling down Peggy's number. She hadn't even had to tell a lie. Or at least, not much of one. She'd simply said that Grandma Alice was in hospital and that she was ringing round as many of her friends as possible to let them know.

Above her, the sky was a cloudless blue – it was hard to imagine the horror that was unfolding in London. She checked the time. She was going to have to hurry if she wanted to catch the train. It had been easy enough getting hold of Peggy's number, but then Dulcie had kept her talking for ages. She hadn't heard from dear Alice in years, she'd said. She often thought of her friend and would love to be in touch again. Maybe they could get together? How was Xanthe doing at school and how were her parents? She'd gone on and on, and the only way Xanthe had managed to get her off the phone in the end was by telling her that she was late for school and promising to ring her back later on with news of her great-grandmother's progress.

It hadn't made things any easier that she'd picked up another hex during the call, even stronger and brighter than the ones she'd seen yesterday evening.

She turned down the hill towards the station. So far everything was going according to plan. All she needed to do now was send a message to Saul and ring Peggy.

Xanthe took out her mobile. *Not in school today*, she texted Saul. *Got another cold. But will be there this afternoon. Promise!*

Next she keyed in Peggy's number: by the look of the area code, Grandma Alice's friend lived somewhere in London. She'd probably be picking up even more hexes than Xanthe was. Her heart lurched as she waited for Peggy to answer. It felt so weird to be phoning another True Witch – someone she'd never met before, but who was so very much like her.

"Hello?" enquired a clear, steady voice.

Xanthe swallowed. "Is that – is that Peggy?"

"Yes. Who is it, please?"

Xanthe turned right at the bottom of the hill and hurried towards the station.

"My name's Xanthe Fox," she said. "I'm Alice Walter's great-granddaughter."

There was a pause.

"Are you indeed?" said Peggy at last. "Well, this *is* a coincidence. I haven't spoken to Alice for years, but I actually tried ringing her last night. Unfortunately, there was no reply."

"She's in hospital," said Xanthe. "She had a fall yesterday afternoon."

"Goodness! Is she all right?"

"I think so. I'm hoping to see her later on. She's fractured her hip and broken one of her arms, but they operated last night, and they reckon she's going to be OK."

There was another brief silence.

"And you're ringing to let me know?" asked Peggy.

Xanthe crossed the road and went into the station.

"Kind of," she said. "That is, not really." She glanced around. No sign of Donna. She was probably waiting on the platform already. "Look, I should probably explain. I'm not just *any* relative of Grandma Alice's. I…"

She tailed off. How on earth was she supposed to tell Peggy the truth about herself in the middle of a busy station concourse?

"Am I to assume you've – er – *taken over* from Alice, Xanthe?"

It was as if a huge weight had lifted from Xanthe's shoulders. "Yes," she replied. "I have. And one of the reasons I'm ringing is to tell you that Grandma Alice has been trying to contact you with some information. Important information about something that took place a couple of weeks ago."

"Information? You're not telling me she knows what happened?"

"What d'you mean?" asked Xanthe nervously.

"Well, if you've taken over from Alice I presume you've been asking yourself exactly the same thing: why we True Witches felt such an incredible energy surge through us the Friday before last. Why we sensed something historic had happened in the witching world."

Xanthe made for the automatic ticket machine and started to feed money into the slot. "Grandma Alice was trying to contact you," she said, lowering her voice to a whisper, "because the thing that happened that Friday happened to *me*."

"To *you*?"

"Yes," murmured Xanthe. She took her ticket and headed for the platform, her eyes darting from side to side as she checked around for Donna. "It's a very long story, but basically there's a Hexing Witch at my school – Donna, her name is – and we had this terrible fight. She hexed me and I – well, I managed to defend myself by summoning fire. Like – like Ethelfreda."

"*What!*" exclaimed Peggy. "But that's incredible! Oh, Xanthe! No wonder we sensed something amazing had happened. Just wait till I tell the others!"

Xanthe felt herself blush. "So you're in touch with some of the other True Witches?"

"A few," said Peggy. "It's been an unexpected bonus to the madness of the last week or so. Until that Friday most of us hadn't even spoken, but now we've begun to network. We got in contact at first because we wanted to pool our thoughts on what might have taken place, but over the last couple of days we've been talking more about what's been going on since." Her voice took on a more serious tone. "You see, we're starting to think the crisis here in London may be the work of a group of Hexing Witches. The hexes we're picking up are like nothing we've ever seen before. They're so strong and bright it's hard to be sure about the surroundings, but we're fairly certain it's water we can see in the background, and yesterday afternoon we thought we glimpsed the reflection of Tower Bridge—"

"Yes," interrupted Xanthe. "That's the other reason I'm ringing. You see, I—"

"I'm afraid the Hexing Witches will have felt something extraordinary happening that Friday, just as we did," rushed on Peggy. "They'll know that the balance of power has shifted somehow, and they'll want to get even. Hexing the Thames must be their idea of revenge. Not that I've ever known them join forces before – they must be well and truly rattled." She paused for a moment. "I suppose we can assume this girl at your school was too ashamed to tell her fellow Hexing Witches what occurred between you?"

"I think so," said Xanthe. "If they knew my identity, they'd have come after me by now, wouldn't they—" She broke off. "Hold on a second, I'm picking up another hex. It's the second I've seen this morning."

Peggy grunted. "Only the second? I'm seeing them all the time. Not that I seem to be making the slightest bit of difference. None of us is. These hexes are way too strong for us to reverse."

Xanthe stiffened. The train was approaching, and out of the corner of one eye she could see

Donna standing amongst the jostling crowd. She was wearing a dark green sweatshirt and jeans, and carrying a small blue rucksack. Her long brown hair was fastened back into a thick plait.

"Peggy, I need to tell you something," she said, cupping her hands round her mobile. "Your hunch about what's going on in London is right. Yesterday I overheard a phone conversation between Donna and one of the other Hexing Witches. Apparently the Thames is very close to bursting its banks and she's agreed to go down there to help with the final push."

There was a sharp intake of breath at the other end of the line.

"Oh my goodness!" exclaimed Peggy. "Then we need to put our heads together and work out what to do! If you can just find out when she's planning to go, I'll scramble together some of the others and get her followed. We're going to have to come face to face with these Hexing Witches if we're to have a hope of doing anything about the situation."

"*Peggy!*" implored Xanthe. "Will you listen to me, *please*? Donna's going to London *today*. *Now*. And I am, too. We're both at the station at Milchester. I thought maybe you could meet me at Victoria and we could follow Donna together…"

"*What!*" Peggy's voice had risen to a squeal.

"*You?* Come to London? Don't even *think* about it! Have you any idea how dangerous it is here right now? Not to mention how dangerous the Hexing Witches are! You must stay away! This is a job for us older True Witches, not you!"

Xanthe frowned. The train was pulling in, and against the noise she could hardly hear what Peggy was saying. "Look, I've got to go. Have a think about my suggestion and text me."

"But *Xanthe*…"

Ending the call, Xanthe switched her mobile on to silent and followed the crowd towards the train. A little further up the platform Donna was already boarding.

She hurried off in the opposite direction and made for the last carriage. She'd keep as far away as possible from Donna during the journey, and then as they approached London she'd make her way up the train and find out where she was sitting.

Because once they pulled into Victoria, she couldn't afford to let her out of her sight.

9.
The Journey

They'd been sitting at Milchester for almost ten minutes now, and there was still no sign of the train leaving the station. Xanthe drummed her fingers against her leg. If they would just get going, perhaps she wouldn't feel so nervous.

She turned her head towards the window. The only seat she'd managed to find was at a table of four, and the lady opposite kept staring at her as if she was about to strike up a conversation. Worse still, she looked vaguely familiar. The last thing she needed right now was a load of busybody questions about what she was doing on a train bound for London on a school day.

"We apologize for the late running of this service," the guard said over the tannoy. "Due to worsening conditions in and around the Thames all trains to London are subject to delay. Current advice is not to travel unless your journey is strictly necessary. Please listen for further announcements."

Xanthe sighed to herself. If anybody's journey was necessary, hers was.

Around her the other passengers had fallen into an uneasy silence. One or two of them were gathering up their belongings and making for the doors.

Xanthe glanced down at her mobile and saw that it was filling up with messages. She hadn't dared take it off silent in case Peggy rang and tried to talk her out of going to London again. A conversation like that would be impossible right now.

At last the guard blew his whistle and there was a jolt as the train pulled away from the station, followed by a hum of relieved murmurs from her fellow passengers. Xanthe felt herself relax a little.

"Don't I know you from somewhere?" The lady opposite was craning forward in her seat and peering at Xanthe over her glasses.

Xanthe flushed. "I–I don't think so," she muttered.

The lady frowned. "I'm *sure* I recognize you. Hang on, aren't you one of the students from the High who comes down to the park after school? Yes, that's right. There's you and that girl with the long black hair. I must have served you both in the café."

Xanthe nodded. So *that's* who she was. One of the ladies who worked in the park café. Trust her to sit down opposite somebody who knew her. She shuffled in her seat, racking her brains for an answer to the question that was surely coming next.

"So come on, then," the lady went on, lowering her voice. "What are you doing on a train to London on a—"

She broke off as her phone rang from the depths of her handbag. A moment later she was talking loudly into it, her question apparently forgotten.

Xanthe breathed a sigh of relief. By the sounds of it, this was going to be a very long conversation. She was safe for a while, at least.

She scanned her messages. There were two from a mobile number she didn't recognize – Peggy's, most probably – and one from Grace as well. She looked at her watch. Five to nine. Registration time. Grace would be heading into weekly assembly soon, and then into lessons.

She clicked on the first message. *OK, then – will get taxi to Victoria and meet you there*, read Peggy's text. *You are NOT doing this on your own. Will be outside ticket barriers wearing brown duffel coat and black beret. P*

Xanthe smiled to herself. Thank goodness Peggy had listened to reason. She scrolled down to the next message.

Am also trying to contact the others in case any of them can get to London in time to meet your train, too.

Xanthe's relief turned to unease. It was sweet of Peggy to want to help, but how on earth did she think a whole group of them was going to follow Donna through London without being noticed? Much better if it was just the pair of them.

PLEASE don't get the others to come to Victoria, she texted back. *I'm sure we can manage fine by ourselves.*

She turned her attention to Grace's message.

Can't believe you're not in today! it read. *What's up? MASSES TO TELL! Chris has asked me out!!!*

Xanthe grinned. It was nice to think about something normal for a change. *Got another cold*, she replied. *That's great about Chris! Where's he taking you?*

A text came back almost immediately.

Skating on Saturday. Are you still meeting Saul this afternoon?

Xanthe's pulse quickened at the thought of her date with Saul. If all went according to plan, she'd be meeting him in less than seven hours.

Yes! Can't cancel on him again! she typed back.

Well, hurry up and get better! And keep me posted about this afternoon. I want to hear ALL about it!

Xanthe's heart beat even faster. The idea that she and Saul might soon be an item was almost too much to imagine. It made her feel sick and scared and happy all at the same time. She gave herself a little shake. She mustn't let her thoughts run away with her like this. Their meeting might turn out to be a total disaster – and in any case, she couldn't afford to think about it right now. For the next few hours she had to concentrate on the task in hand.

Her phone pinged with another message from Peggy.

OK. Will put the others on standby. Maybe they could meet us once we've tracked the HWs down. Trying to get hold of taxi firm now…

Xanthe looked out of the window. The train had picked up speed and the countryside was rushing past in a greenish-brown blur.

"I don't know, love," the lady from the café was saying into her mobile. "I think we're just a bit delayed, that's all." There was a pause. "Well, I'll see what happens when I get to Victoria. If they end up closing the Underground, I'll have to get a bus or a taxi."

Xanthe swallowed. She hadn't thought what she'd do if the Underground was closed. Following Donna through London on a bus would be much more difficult than on the tube, and a taxi would be almost impossible.

Another X swam in front of her eyes and she frowned. This was even bigger and brighter than the one she'd seen at the station, and there was no questioning its watery surroundings. The Hexing Witches' power was obviously growing by the minute.

Knowing by now that she was powerless to do anything about the hex, she shut her eyes to blot out the shape and leaned her head to one side. At least this way she'd be spared any more for a while. And with luck Mrs Nosey opposite would take the hint and leave her alone once she'd finished her call.

For another twenty minutes or so she would pretend to be a perfectly normal passenger.

The tannoy crackled into life and Xanthe jumped in her seat.

"This train will shortly be arriving at Victoria," announced the guard. "Please take care when leaving the train and remember to take all your belongings with you. Passengers are advised that due to current conditions the Underground is operating a severely restricted service."

Xanthe leaped to her feet. They were nearly there and she hadn't even begun to look for Donna! The movement of the train must have lulled her into a doze.

The lady opposite looked up at her. "It's all right," she said. "There's no rush. We'll be another few minutes at least." She winked. "You never answered my question. You never told me what you were doing on a train to London on a school day."

Xanthe flushed. She squeezed past the person on her left and took down her rucksack from the overhead rack. Then she hovered in the aisle for a moment before turning and hurrying towards the doors leading to the next carriage. She didn't *have* to answer the lady's stupid question, did she? What she did and didn't do was no one's business but hers.

She glanced down at her mobile to see two more texts from Peggy.

Can't see any of the others getting to London today, the first one read. *Travel network rapidly disintegrating. You're lucky to have got a train at all.*

Xanthe frowned. It was a relief to hear she wasn't about to get a full-on welcoming committee at the station, but she didn't like the sound of the other part of Peggy's text. If the travel network was disintegrating, that probably meant the Hexing Witches were getting dangerously close to their goal of flooding London. She looked at the second message.

Can't get a taxi for love nor money. And the buses are going nowhere. If I don't make it in time, promise me you won't track Donna by yourself. IT'S TOO DANGEROUS. Just get on the first train home.

Xanthe rolled her eyes. She hadn't come all this way to turn back the moment she got to London. She was following Donna with or without Peggy — she had to. Slipping her mobile into her pocket, she went through into the next carriage, scanning the seats in front of her. She probably had a bit further to go before she found where Donna was sitting, but she wasn't taking any chances.

Inside the carriage, people were preparing to leave, standing up to put on their coats and reaching for their luggage. Xanthe edged past them, blushing and apologizing.

Her stomach knotted as she approached the next set of interconnecting doors. She had to be careful. If Donna caught sight of her, things could get very awkward.

The train jerked to a halt, and for a moment she thought they had already arrived at Victoria. Then she noticed that the other passengers were peering out of the windows and pointing at something below. Some of them were taking pictures on their phones.

Xanthe followed their gaze and her eyes widened. Beneath them lay the river, a swollen mass of choppy greyness, littered with pieces of debris that circled and eddied with the currents. She felt for her locket. This was far worse than the pictures she'd seen on TV, far worse than anything she'd *ever* seen. Helicopters whirred overhead and the air was shrill with the wail of police sirens.

"It's more like a sea than a river!" exclaimed an elderly gentleman. "Those banks won't hold out much longer, surely!"

The lady beside him shuddered. "You wouldn't survive two minutes in there," she said. "I wish I'd listened to my instincts and stayed at home."

Xanthe forced herself to look away. With everyone's attention diverted, this was as good a chance as any to make her way further down the train. Donna would almost certainly be staring at the Thames along with the rest of them, admiring the handiwork of the other Hexing Witches.

She inched into the next carriage, scouring the heads and faces of the people in front of her. And then her heart missed a beat. There she was! About halfway down, sitting next to a young man in a leather jacket, the faintest of smiles playing on her lips as she looked at the seething waters.

Xanthe ducked behind a tall gentleman with a suitcase and held her breath, willing Donna to keep her focus on the river. From here she had the perfect view of her.

The train lurched forward, and suddenly the aisle was filled with passengers heading for the doors.

Everyone began talking to one another, exclaiming over the state of the river and sharing their worries at the likely disruption to their onward journeys.

Xanthe stumbled as somebody shoved past her, and it was a moment before she regained her balance. When she looked up again, she realized she had completely lost sight of Donna. However much she craned her neck to catch a glimpse of the people further up the carriage, all she could see was a wall of coats and cases.

Panic seized her. Once they stopped at Victoria and passengers started pouring out on to the platform, she wouldn't stand a chance of spotting Donna. She had to find her again before she left the train…

But already they were pulling into the station and the guard was announcing their arrival. The wall of coats began to move forward and Xanthe had to fight back the urge to push everybody to one side and lunge for the doors.

This wasn't how she'd planned things at all.

10.
Underground

Xanthe stood under the departure boards, her heart racing. Her eyes swept the concourse, taking in the little shops and cafés, the flower stall, the central information point, the entrance to the Underground, desperate for a glimpse of Donna's brown plait. Maybe she was still here somewhere... Maybe she'd stopped to get some food before heading for the tube...

Please be here, she begged silently. *Please!*

The station was packed. People were rushing about all over the place, most swarming towards the steps leading down to the Underground, some hurrying outside to the bus station, others gazing up at the arrival and departure boards, every one of which showed trains cancelled or seriously delayed.

Xanthe ran her fingers through her short chestnut hair. She'd done her best to find Donna once she was on the platform, dodging in and out of the crowds like a thing possessed. But there'd been a hold-up at the ticket barriers and by the time she'd made it on to the concourse, there was no sign of her and she'd wanted to burst into tears. Peggy wasn't anywhere to be seen, either – she obviously hadn't managed to get a taxi.

"Don't just stand there," she muttered under her breath, as another X appeared before her eyes. "You've got to *do* something."

She blinked away the shape and made her way towards the entrance to the Underground.

"Attention London Underground passengers," announced a voice over the tannoy, as she joined the crowd waiting to go down the steps. "All lines are operating a severely restricted service. Passengers are advised to seek alternative methods of transport wherever possible."

And now another announcement was booming through the concourse. "The delayed 9.14 to Milchester will depart from Platform Six in fifteen minutes. Would all passengers for this service make their way to the ticket barriers."

Xanthe glanced over her shoulder at the departure boards. There it was, in amongst all the cancelled and delayed notices, in bright orange: "TRAIN NOW BOARDING." She fought back the urge to turn round and get on the train. She had to keep searching for Donna. She *had* to. She was the True Witches' only hope.

She pushed on towards the Underground entrance, her eyes flitting from side to side.

And then she stopped dead.

Standing to one side of the steps, her pale face bent over a street map of London, was Donna.

At long last things seemed to be going her way. So far she'd managed to shadow Donna down the steps to the Underground, through the ticket barriers and on to the escalators without being spotted.

Xanthe offered up a silent prayer. Thank goodness she'd had the sense to buy a travelcard at Milchester. Queuing at the ticket machines would have meant losing Donna again for sure.

She followed her on to the eastbound platform of the District and Circle Lines and stood behind the sea of passengers waiting for a train. It was hot down here, and impossibly crowded. The edge of someone's briefcase kept jabbing into her leg, and she could smell the foul breath of the man standing behind her. But she didn't care. Her plans were back on track, and that was all that mattered.

After what felt like ages, a low rumble sounded in the distance and built to a roar as a train approached the station. It screeched to a halt and the doors slid open – the next moment everyone was surging forward, colliding with people attempting to get off.

"Stand away from the platform edge!" bellowed the guard. "Let passengers off the train first!"

Xanthe shrank back against the man with bad breath. The entire contents of the train seemed to be spilling towards her, scattering the waiting crowd and almost hiding Donna from view. She pursed her lips. There was no way she was going to lose her twice.

At last the train emptied of departing passengers and people began to board. Xanthe shuffled along, not once taking her eyes off Donna.

"Move right down inside the carriages!" instructed the guard.

Xanthe's stomach lurched. What if she couldn't get on to the train? What if she got left behind? She pushed forward, all manners forgotten, until she was so close to Donna she could almost have reached out and touched her.

At that moment Donna twisted round to adjust one of the shoulder-straps on her rucksack – and for a heart-stopping second Xanthe thought she had seen her. She ducked to one side and held her breath, but when she looked again she saw that Donna had turned back to face the train and was getting ready to board.

Xanthe squeezed on after her and wedged herself behind a couple of businessmen in dark suits. Almost at once the doors slid shut. She just had time to grab the nearest handrail, and then the train jerked away from the station and hurtled into the darkness.

So far they had stopped at six stations, and still there was no sign they were about to get off. Xanthe moved very slightly to her left and risked a quick glance at Donna's pale face, less than two metres away from her. She had opened up her map again, and was poring over it, a frown etched into her forehead. Wherever it was they were heading, she clearly wasn't too confident of finding the way.

Xanthe ducked back behind the group of women now standing in front of her. The two businessmen had got off at the last stop, along with quite a few other passengers, and the carriage was a lot less full. Of course, this had its advantages: it was easier to breathe, for one thing, and it meant she wasn't constantly being elbowed in the ribs or having her feet trodden on. But mainly it made life much more difficult – with fewer people to lurk behind she risked Donna seeing her at any second. And it didn't help that there were Xs popping up in front of her eyes all the time, either.

The train suddenly ground to a halt in the middle of the tunnel. People looked up from their books and newspapers and glanced around. The next moment the lights dimmed, then went out altogether.

A little boy started to whimper.

"It's all right, sweetheart," murmured his mother in soothing tones. "It's nothing to worry about. I'm sure they'll come back on soon."

Xanthe's heart thumped against her chest. She didn't like this one bit. What on earth was she *doing* down here, standing in almost total darkness not far from someone who'd only recently tried to leave her stranded at the bottom of an icy lake? She was supposed to be in lessons with Grace, for goodness' sake. If her parents could see her now they'd have a fit. As for Grandma Alice – well, the other day she hadn't even wanted her to walk home by herself.

She felt a stab of guilt. She really ought to ring Peggy and let her know where she was. Perhaps the old lady had at last got hold of a taxi and they could arrange a new rendezvous. Or maybe she'd finally managed to rally some of the other True Witches. It would be wonderful to have some support.

She'd phone Peggy the moment she got out of the Underground. *If* she got out of the Underground.

After what seemed like ages, the lights flickered back on and the train limped off down the tunnel. A few minutes later it shuddered to a standstill at the next station.

The doors opened, but no one got on. Instead the crowd on the platform appeared to be turning round and heading for the exit. Some of them were running.

"Due to worsening conditions in and around the Thames, the capital has been placed on high alert," announced the guard. "All services on the London Underground have been suspended until further notice. Please vacate this train immediately and leave by the nearest available exit."

Xanthe stood rooted to the spot. The authorities only put places on high alert in really serious circumstances, didn't they? Usually when people's lives were at risk. She tried to steady her breathing. It could only mean one thing: with all the reinforcements they had drafted in, the Hexing Witches were now working at lightning speed.

Around her the other passengers were jumping to their feet and making for the doors.

"I knew it," one lady muttered to her companion, as she hurried off the train. "I *knew* we shouldn't have come to London today. That river's going to burst its banks – and I don't want to be anywhere near it when it does."

As Xanthe followed Donna on to the platform, she saw the look in her eyes. She'd seen her wear the same expression before – on the afternoon they had faced each other down at the boathouse, before they had wrestled each other into the lake.

It was the look of triumph.

11.
Overground

Outside the Underground station, Xanthe skirted round a team of officials in fluorescent yellow jackets and glanced up. Five or six helicopters were circling overhead, splitting the air with their heavy droning sound.

Not far off, Donna was leaning against some railings, frowning over her map. She looked even less sure of where she was heading than she had done earlier. And who could blame her? She'd almost certainly been banking on getting as close to her destination by tube as she could. Now she was going to have to finish the journey on foot.

Xanthe edged behind the officials and kept her head down. One of them was speaking through a tannoy to the people coming out of the station.

"Make your way towards the bus stops on the Strand!" he bellowed. "All buses are heading north, so just board the first one available and get as far away from the river as possible."

Xanthe took out her mobile and checked the screen. Since she'd been down in the Underground, Peggy had left her no fewer than seven texts – and they all said pretty much the same thing: *Catch the first train home! Don't follow Donna! Get out of London now!*

She reached into her jeans pocket and closed her hand round her locket. As soon as Donna got moving, she would ring Peggy and tell her what was going on. What with the helicopters and the tannoy and the general hubbub all around her, she needn't worry about being overheard.

A few minutes later Donna set off in the direction of the Strand, her nose still buried in the map. She'd obviously decided to look as though she was obeying official advice for now, then sneak back towards the river when there were fewer eyes on her. Xanthe followed her at a safe distance and dialled Peggy's number.

The old lady answered at once. "*Xanthe!* Oh, thank goodness! Are you all right?"

"I'm fine. I had a bit of a problem at Victoria, and I—"

"I've been out of my *mind* with worry!" interrupted Peggy. "I've been practically tearing my hair out."

"I'm really sorry." Xanthe quickened her pace as Donna turned right on to the Strand, which was heaving with people trying to board the buses. "Like I said, I had a problem at Victoria. I lost Donna for a while, but then I found her again and followed her into the Underground…"

"*Followed* her? Into the *Underground*! But didn't you get my last text? I told you to catch the first train back to Milchester."

"Look, Peggy, I know we were hoping to shadow Donna together, but things have changed."

"Of course things have changed! The capital's been put on high alert! Where are you now, for heaven's sake?"

"Heading up the Strand. They've closed the Underground, so I guess we'll have to walk the rest of the way."

"But I don't want you going anywhere *near* those Hexing Witches!" exclaimed Peggy.

There was a brief pause.

"Have you heard back from any of the others?" demanded Xanthe. "Is there a chance some of them might be able to meet me if I can find out where the Hexing Witches are operating from?"

"No," said Peggy shortly. "No chance at all. They

simply can't get to London. The authorities have blocked all the routes in."

Xanthe chewed her lip. She mustn't show Peggy how scared she was feeling. "Then can't you see?" she said. "It's me or no one." A shiver snaked down her spine. "There's no point trying to stop me, Peggy. I'm following Donna, and that's that."

There was a very long silence at the other end of the line.

"And what will you do when you get there?" said Peggy at last.

Xanthe hung back as Donna stopped beside a huge white church and consulted her map. "I'm not exactly sure. It depends what I find, I suppose. But I'll think of something. I dealt with Donna at the boathouse, didn't I? It's not like I've never faced a Hexing Witch before."

"But that was only one of them. And a very young one at that. By the look of the hexes we're picking up, I'd guess there's a fair few of them at work down there. It's a totally different situation."

Xanthe blinked away another X and followed Donna down a much narrower street to one side of the church. They were obviously heading back towards the river. "I won't take any stupid risks, I promise. I'll be careful."

There was another pause.

"In which case," said Peggy, "if there really is no way I can persuade you to change your mind, I'd better try and get hold of that taxi firm again and come and meet you. Text me regularly so I can keep track of you – and when you get there, *wait* for me. We'll stand a much better chance of defeating those witches together."

"OK," said Xanthe. Relief rushed through her. Perhaps – just perhaps – she wasn't going to have to face the Hexing Witches on her own after all. "That sounds like a plan—" She broke off. Donna had just turned down another road, and the crowds and the noise seemed suddenly to have melted away. "I've got to go," she whispered. "I'll be in touch."

Ringing off, she put her mobile back into her pocket and hurried after Donna.

Xanthe checked her watch. She'd been tracking Donna for over half an hour and most of the roads were now lined with vast, empty-looking warehouses. Sandbags stood propped against doorways and the air was filled with an eerie stillness, broken only by the scream of nearby sirens and the whirring of helicopters overhead.

The streets were almost completely deserted – since ending her call with Peggy she'd only seen a handful of people, and they had been hurrying away in the opposite direction. Of course, this made following Donna much harder; though she was careful to keep a good distance between them, she still felt that at any moment she might have to spring back and flatten herself against a wall. Luckily for her, Donna hadn't looked round once. She'd paused several times to check her map, but apart from that she'd marched straight on.

Xanthe peered through the gap between the two warehouses on her right; from here she could just make out a snatch of heaving river, grey and menacing beneath the pale blue sky. Since turning off the Strand, Donna seemed to have grown in confidence, using every backstreet she could find to zigzag her way towards the Thames. Now she stopped at a crossroads and gazed about her, frowning.

Xanthe's heart raced. Perhaps this was it. Perhaps they were here at last. She glanced up at the windows on the other side of the street, half expecting to see a line of witchy-looking figures glaring down at her, but the dark panes of glass stared back at her like unseeing eyes, revealing nothing.

Donna was bending over her map again, turning it this way and that. She took a few steps to the right, then changed her mind and returned to her original spot.

A helicopter circled low above them and Xanthe was seized by the sudden impulse to take advantage of the noise and ring Peggy. As instructed, she'd been texting every five minutes or so to tell her where she was, but right now what she wanted more than anything else was to hear another human voice – the voice of someone who understood the danger she was in.

She pressed herself against the nearest wall and took out her mobile.

"Peggy," she murmured. "It's me."

"Xanthe! Where are you now?"

Xanthe cupped her hand round the phone.

"I'm not sure exactly," she said, raising her voice over the deafening throb of the helicopter. "I can't read any street signs from here. But there are hexes coming at me all the time, and I can see the river. Donna's stopped at a crossroads and doesn't seem to know where to go next. I reckon we must be nearly there. Still no luck with a taxi?"

Peggy sighed. "No. The line's constantly engaged. It seems the whole of London's trying to get one."

Xanthe felt her jaw tighten. It really did look like she was on her own. "Have … have there been any more news updates on the river?"

"Only that the water levels are still rising. Officials are saying it can't be more than an hour before the banks

113

burst. They're even talking about drafting in the army."

"The *army*?" Xanthe stiffened. "Hold on, Donna's on the move again. I'd better go…"

"Wait a minute!" cried Peggy. "I want to know exactly where you are. Tell me which street you're on."

Xanthe crossed the road after Donna, screwing up her eyes to read the sign ahead of her. The helicopter was flying off now, leaving in its wake an ominous hush. "I'm on Gregory Street," she whispered. "I…"

She frowned down at her phone. The line had gone dead and the words *No network coverage* had appeared on the screen. Sighing to herself, she slipped her mobile back in her pocket and looked up the street once more.

Her blood ran cold.

In the time it had taken to glance at her phone, Donna had vanished.

12.
Hexing Witch HQ

Xanthe fought back another hex and stared around wildly. Where on earth had Donna gone? Two seconds ago she'd been right in front of her, and now she'd disappeared.

As far as she could see, there were no side roads leading off Gregory Street. It looked like a solid row of warehouses, just like the previous street had been. Which meant Donna must have slipped inside a building. Perhaps at this very moment another Hexing Witch was ushering her inside and closing the door behind her.

She broke into a run. If she was lucky, she might hear them talking or pick up some movement at a window.

A second later she was skidding to a halt.

There she was, panicking again. What if Donna was standing inside the entrance to the headquarters, still waiting to be let in? What if the door swung open just as she went past? The last thing she wanted to do was run headlong into the Hexing Witches' clutches. She needed to catch them unawares.

Xanthe crept down the street, scanning the windows of each building she approached and listening at every doorway – but she could see nothing, and the only sound was the whirring of the retreating helicopter and the familiar wail of police sirens.

She frowned to herself. She must be halfway along Gregory Street by now – easily level with the place she had last seen Donna – but there was no sign of any activity. What was more, all the entrances were either boarded up or covered by metal grilles. Surely she would have heard the noise of one of these being removed if Donna had been let in somewhere? It didn't make sense.

She stumbled over a pile of litter lying in the middle of the pavement and gave it a vicious kick. It looked like she'd let Donna slip through her fingers at the last moment.

A gust of wind tugged at the scattered litter and sent it skittering down the street in front of her.

And that was when she saw it, no more than a couple of metres away to her right – the entrance to an alleyway, hardly wide enough for two people to pass each other.

She rushed towards it, her spirits soaring, then drew back. At the end of the alleyway, bending to tie the laces of her trainers, her body turned slightly to one side, was the one person she wanted to see.

Xanthe stood just short of the entrance, praying she hadn't been spotted. Only when Donna had got to her feet and her blue rucksack had disappeared round the corner did she dare to move, slowly at first, then faster and faster, her heart pounding against her chest.

She was nearly at the end of the alleyway when she stiffened. Xs were flashing up in front of her eyes every few seconds now, and against the background noise of helicopters and sirens, she could hear the rushing and splashing of water. But there was another sound, too – the unmistakable murmur of Donna's voice.

Xanthe peered round the corner. Donna was standing in a narrow street opposite a huge old warehouse, talking into her phone. Evidently the mobile signal had returned.

She strained her ears to hear what she was saying,

but the words were too muffled. Perhaps they still had a way to go, and she was asking for directions. Or maybe she'd changed her mind about joining the other witches and was phoning them with an excuse. She certainly seemed to have a lot to say – she was gabbling away at breakneck speed and her face was unusually flushed.

At last she finished the call and put her phone in her pocket. Xanthe held her breath, waiting for Donna either to carry on walking or to return to the alleyway – but she did neither. Instead she stood quite still, her head tilted slightly to one side, not once taking her eyes off the door to the warehouse in front of her.

It happened so fast Xanthe had no time to react. One minute Donna was standing by herself in the middle of the narrow street and the next the door to the warehouse was bursting open and a group of women was streaming out towards her.

"She's over there!" shouted Donna, turning round and pointing to the alleyway.

Xanthe stood rooted to the spot, the truth slamming into her. *She'd been set up!* Donna had known she was there all the time! She had lured her here and like a fool she had walked straight into the trap!

She stared open-mouthed as the women rushed in her direction. Sense told her that in a few seconds they would be upon her, but her body refused to move. Time seemed to have slowed right down and all she could do was stand and watch. The Xs had stopped appearing, and as the witches approached she took in every detail – there had to be at least ten of them and their faces were purple with anger: there was a red-headed woman at the front; a younger one behind her in jeans and a dark green sweater; a tall, fair one in a smart pin-striped skirt, who seemed to have dressed more for a morning in the office than a day in a warehouse attempting to flood London. None of them looked in the least as she'd imagined they would. But then, what had she been expecting? A collection of old hags in robes and pointy black hats? Honestly, she was as bad as her classmates.

Too late her brain snapped into action. Xanthe made to run back up the alleyway, but already the red-headed witch at the front of the pack was wrestling her to the ground.

"Let's see then, shall we?" she murmured, holding Xanthe down and pushing her face roughly to one side. "Let's see if this is true."

She bent to examine the back of Xanthe's neck, then twisted round to address the rest of the witches who had gathered behind her.

"Donna's right!" she breathed. "She *is* a True Witch. She's got the mark on her neck."

There was a moment's silence, followed by an explosion of cries. "She's a True Witch! She's a True Witch! Donna was telling the truth!" Some of the women were clutching each other, their eyes wide; others had moved in closer to get a better look. Every one of them was glaring down at Xanthe.

Under the redhead's grip, Xanthe forced herself to return their gaze. A little to the left of the group she could see Donna, smirking.

The redhead turned to Donna. "So go on, then," she said. "You said on the phone just now that you'd lured a True Witch down here. But how did you do it? Do you *know* her or something?"

Donna smiled coyly. "She goes to my school. I discovered she was a True Witch a couple of weeks ago and started trying out my hexing skills on her." Her smile began to falter. "Then the Friday before last we had a massive fight in the lake in our local park. Once we were out of the water, she – well, she managed to reverse the hex I was sparking on her by summoning fire."

The Hexing Witches gasped.

"By summoning *what*?" exclaimed the redhead.

Donna looked down at the ground. The smile

had disappeared completely from her face. "Fire," she whispered. "Like – like Ethelfreda did. That's why I decided to pay her back and lead her here."

The redhead turned to Xanthe. She seemed to be having trouble finding her voice.

"So it was you who changed everything the other week, was it?" she murmured at last, digging her nails into Xanthe's shoulders. "It was you who dared to challenge one of our kind?" Xanthe said nothing. The witch's face was so close that she could feel the warmth of her breath on her skin. "Well, don't think you can get away with it. The tables have turned now, haven't they? I think you might just regret your moment of glory."

The others drew closer, nodding and muttering to one another. The woman in the pin-striped skirt said something to the witch beside her, and a chant started up, softly at first, then louder and louder. "Hex her!" they cried. "Hex her! Hex her! Hex her!"

Xanthe struggled to free herself. She had to get away. She must have been mad to have ever thought she could stand a chance against this lot. She glanced over her shoulder, praying that Peggy might suddenly appear and rescue her – but the rest of the alleyway was deserted.

"What d'you think you're doing?" shrieked a voice, cutting through the noise. "Leaving me alone like that! I can't flood London by myself!"

The witches fell silent and turned as one. Behind them stood a woman in a silvery-grey headscarf – older than the rest, with deep lines etched into her forehead. She wore thick-rimmed glasses and was leaning on a walking-stick.

"You've lost us valuable time!" she went on. "The water levels have dropped already. What we're attempting requires constant effort – there can't be any let-up, not even for a few seconds."

Xanthe glanced from the redhead to the newcomer, and felt the air crackle between them.

"But, Michaela," said the redhead at last, her cheeks burning, "what else could we have done? We had to check out the girl, didn't we? And she's definitely a True Witch. I've seen the mark." She paused for breath before rushing on. "And wait until you hear *this*! Apparently she summoned fire when Donna here tried to hex her the other week. *She's* the reason the balance of power tipped against us that Friday. *She's* the reason we got so angry and decided to come down here and hex the Thames."

Michaela looked at Xanthe and narrowed her eyes. "Well, well, well," she murmured. "It seems we've bagged ourselves a very nice little catch." She prodded Xanthe hard with her stick before returning her attention to the redhead. "But it only needed one of you to go and get her. You didn't *all* have to abandon me." She glowered round at the group of witches. "And whatever you do, don't go wasting your energies hexing her! Right now we must concentrate on the river! On getting those banks to burst!"

"But what are we going to do with her?" asked the redhead. "We can't just let her go!"

Michaela smashed her stick down on the ground. "Did I say anything about letting her go? I'm hardly going to pass up on the opportunity of getting even with the True Witch responsible for challenging our powers. But we can deal with her later. Once we've achieved our goal. For now we'll just have to take her with us to the banks."

"To the banks?"

Michaela nodded. "It's no good carrying on as we have been. We haven't made that much progress in the last half-hour, have we? The closer we get to flooding the river, the harder it seems to get. We've got to get nearer to the water. Much nearer."

The other women eyed each other.

"But what if the banks burst while we're down there?" murmured the witch in the pin-striped skirt. "What if we're swept away?"

Michaela snorted. "That won't happen," she said. "We'll wait till the last minute and then head back to the warehouse and finish it from there. We'll be safe on the top floor, and our provisions will last us for days if necessary. Now come on! Bring the girl and follow me to the river. There's not a moment to lose!"

She turned to go, then glanced back over her shoulder at Donna. "When we get to the banks, you're to stay with our guest. You brought her here, so it's only fair you should have that privilege. Hold her down in any way you like, and don't spare her any pain – but whatever you do, keep your eyes focused on the Thames. We need all the help we can get."

Xanthe's heart leaped. Maybe there was a way out of this after all. If she just had Donna to contend with, she might be able to get away while the other witches were hexing the river. Especially if Donna had to keep her eyes fixed on the Thames.

"B-but what if she tries reversing our hexes?" stammered Donna.

Michaela gave a throaty laugh. "She can try all she likes, but she won't succeed. Not unless she actually jumps into the water, and I can't see her risking that. She might be a witch, but that river's no place for anyone. The currents will be worse than lethal." She gave a twisted grin. "But if it'll make you happier, blindfold her. And tie her hands behind her back for good measure. She won't get up to any mischief then, will she?"

And with that she planted her stick firmly in front of her and limped off towards the river.

13.
On the Banks of the Thames

Xanthe lay slumped against a mooring post, her legs stretched out before her.

She bit her lip. The piece of rope that had been used to tie her hands together was cutting into her wrists, and it was all she could do not to cry out in pain. She would hold back her tears, though. She'd watched as Donna had tightened the knot and seen the pleasure in her face – there was no way she was going to add to her delight by letting her know how much it hurt.

If only she could see, it wouldn't be so bad. But Donna had followed Michaela's suggestion and blindfolded her, too. The older witch had offered up her scarf for the job, and the last thing Xanthe had seen before it had been wound round her head was Michaela's shock of white hair falling to her shoulders in long, greasy streaks. She looked almost like a witch from a storybook.

Her mind flitted over the events of the past few minutes. Back in the alleyway, the red-headed Hexing Witch had hauled her to her feet and dragged her after the others, past the warehouse and down another narrow passage. At the end of that they had turned a corner and squeezed through some railings – and there, no more than a stone's throw in front of them, was the Thames, frothing and churning beneath a cloudless blue sky.

In a fraction of a second Xanthe had taken in the whole scene: the angry waves slapping against the banks, sending plumes of spray high into the air; the scummy surface, littered with plastic bottles and bits of wood and metal; the nearby cluster of abandoned barges bashing into one another at the water's edge; the helicopters flying overhead. Not far downstream Tower Bridge straddled the river – the centrepiece of a picture postcard of London gone wrong.

The next moment Michaela had started shouting at the other Hexing Witches to hurry up and get into line along the bank – all except Donna, whose job it had been to tie her hands and blindfold her. The riverbank had been a hive of activity as the witches jostled for position, bickering over the best place to stand and concentrating their gazes on the water seething just below their feet.

She was wrenched from her thoughts by the sound of a voice hissing in her ear.

"You thought you were so clever, didn't you?" murmured Donna. "Catching the train to London and shadowing me through the streets like a real detective. Not that you'd ever have got here if I hadn't given you a helping hand. Honestly! The number of times I had to wait for you to catch up!"

Xanthe said nothing. She wrinkled up her nose behind the blindfold and tried not to gag at the sickly stench of Michaela's perfume, which seemed to have found its way into every thread of the material.

From the edge of the river, the Hexing Witches gave a whoop of delight.

"The water levels are rising again!" Michaela cried. "It won't be long now! Come on, let's jump aboard that barge – we'll be even closer then." Xanthe heard the clattering of feet on wooden boards as the women clambered on to one of the moored barges she had seen earlier.

"It was easy to trick you into coming down here," Donna gloated, when the witches had fallen silent once more. "You were *so* gullible. D'you remember me talking on my phone in the library? All that fuss I made hiding behind the encyclopedia? That was just me making sure I had your full attention. I wasn't actually *speaking* to anyone. I didn't even have my mobile switched on. But I'd guessed from your face in English that you'd started picking up hexes, and it seemed like the perfect time to put my plan into action." She laughed. "Of course, I knew you'd get the wrong end of the stick completely. I knew you'd think there must be Hexing Witches in Milchester hatching a plot against *you* – but that was fine by me. At that point I just wanted to worry you, and to put you on the alert for more phone calls."

Xanthe's stomach knotted. What she would have given right now to have shoved Donna in the heaving river. But with her hands tied and her eyes blindfolded, she was as good as useless.

"And you fell for it again the very next day. In Miss Pimm's maths class I sent myself a text while she was rabbiting on about the new topic. It was a bit of a risk, but I'd put the settings on low and just hoped she wouldn't hear my mobile beeping. I guessed *you'd* hear it, though. And I guessed you'd follow me out of the room, too. I just had to wait till you came down the corridor, then all I had to do was strike up another imaginary conversation."

Xanthe remembered the moment she had crept towards the cloakroom and heard Donna's voice. She'd been so certain she was about to hear details of a revenge plot aimed at her. How stupid had she been!

"I knew it wouldn't take much to get you to follow me to London," said Donna. "Xanthe the heroine strikes again. I knew you wouldn't be able to resist—"

She broke off as Michaela shouted at her from the barge. "Donna! Stop talking to the girl and concentrate on hexing the river! We may not have much longer! I think that helicopter might have spotted us!"

Xanthe leaned against the mooring post, desperate to get herself out of this nightmare situation. "So none of the other Hexing Witches was in on this plan to lure me here?" she asked. "You didn't tell anyone about what had happened between us down at the boathouse until today? Not even your ancestor?"

There was a short pause before Donna replied. "You must be joking," she murmured. "I have got a *bit* of pride. They knew I was coming down to London to help, but they didn't know anything about you till a few minutes ago, when I phoned them from outside the warehouse. I wanted to surprise them. Of course, they realized *something* had occurred that Friday afternoon; they sensed the change in the balance of power – my ancestor told me that. That's why they hatched a plan to come down and flood London – they wanted to get even with the True Witches and show their strength. But they didn't know *what* had taken place, or who it had happened to." Donna's voice dropped even lower as she went on. "And there's something they *still* don't know about. Something they'll discover soon enough, but which I want to get my hands on first."

"And what's that?" muttered Xanthe.

"Your locket, of course. I want to be the one to strip you of your powers. And I want it as my trophy for luring you down here, too. The others will know you'll have inherited some sort of heirloom from your ancestor, but they're too busy to think about that now. I'm sure once they've succeeded in flooding the river they'll be keen enough to find it and take it off you, but I think I've earned the right to do that, don't you? Let's face it, there's nothing you can do against so many Hexing Witches, is there? You might as well give in. And if you tell me where it is without making a fuss, I might just loosen that rope a little."

Xanthe stiffened. She'd forgotten all about her locket. It was inside the back pocket of her jeans with her purse, just inches from where Donna was standing. She kept very still and said nothing.

"I see," muttered Donna. "Well, if that's how you want to play it, I'll have to look for it myself."

She began tugging at Xanthe's rucksack, then pulled away as Michaela's voice cut through the air once more.

"Donna! Didn't you hear me? Leave the girl alone and come here! *Now!* Before I have to drag you over."

Donna's voice hissed into Xanthe's ear one final time. "I've not finished with you yet," she said. "I'll be back for that locket."

There was the sound of footsteps as Donna went to join the other witches on the barge.

"We've nearly cracked it," Michaela went on. "But that helicopter's definitely seen us, so let's hex the river from here for another few minutes, then go back to the warehouse and try and finish things off from there."

Xanthe chewed her lip. An idea was forming in her head, an idea so crazy she could scarcely believe she was even considering it. But she couldn't just stay here and await her fate, and it was clear Peggy wasn't about to turn up and rescue her. If she was going to escape, she would have to do it on her own.

She wriggled up the mooring post until she was sitting bolt upright. With her hands tied behind her back and Michaela's headscarf over her eyes, she'd be putting herself in terrible danger, but right now it was the only plan she could think of. And it might just mean she could do something about the river, too.

Stumbling to her feet, she began to move forward. She ran until the ground gave way beneath her and she was running on nothing but thin air ... and then she plunged into the seething Thames and sank beneath its scummy surface.

It was much worse than it had been in the lake. At least there the water had been still and she had felt only tendrils of weed brushing against her body. Here there were currents pulling her in every direction, and the river seemed to be teeming with bits of rubbish.

She did have one advantage this time, though – she knew that she could breathe down here. There was no need for her to hold her breath as she had done before. She could open her mouth and take in huge gulps of water, safe in the knowledge that her body would treat it exactly like air. It was one of the perks of her peculiar inheritance – witches could breathe underwater.

She couldn't feel the cold, either – and it was a good thing, too. By now any ordinary mortal would have died of hypothermia. To her, the river felt as warm as the public swimming pool in Milchester.

Something hurled itself against her right shin, something which felt like a sheet of metal, and she cried out in pain, starting at the sound of her own voice. The next moment she had caught the object between her knees and was arching backward, positioning the rope that bound her wrists over the edge of the metal sheet and moving her arms to and fro. A few seconds later the rope snapped in two and her hands sprang apart.

Xanthe reached up and tore off the blindfold.

She blinked in her new surroundings. It was another world beneath the surface of the Thames – a dark, surprising world where debris of every shape and size loomed towards her, only to disappear a moment later into the shadows. A little way below her she could see the outline of an upturned boat, and everywhere she looked there were glowing Xs.

This was her chance to do something about the hexes. Surely she could bring the water level down now she was actually in the river…

She tried to focus her attention on the closest of the Xs, but the currents pulled her this way and that, and it was impossible to keep still. What was more, she was becoming distracted by a stinging sensation in her shin. Though it was too dark to see, she sensed that blood was seeping through her jeans where the sheet of metal had cut into her.

Her pulse began to quicken. She might be immune to the cold, and she could breathe OK, but that didn't mean she was invincible. What with the shifting currents and her injured leg, it wouldn't be long before she started to grow weak.

She tried to organize her thoughts. Her best bet was probably to swim a little further downstream and pull herself to safety away from the prying eyes of the Hexing Witches.

Quickly, she loosened the knot in Michaela's headscarf and tied it round her shin. With any luck that would be enough to stem the blood for a while. She peered through the dark water, trying to get her bearings, but everywhere she looked was a mass of confusing shadows; she had twisted and turned with the currents so much that she had completely lost sight of the edge of the river.

Fighting back a growing sense of panic, Xanthe swam towards the largest of the shadows, praying that she was heading for the riverbank – but a few metres on she hit another current that whipped at her limbs and dragged her off in the opposite direction.

She strained against it, but the force was too strong. A moment later it had taken hold of her entirely and she felt herself being swept out into the middle of the churning river, Michaela's mocking words resounding in her ears – *She might be a witch, but that river's no place for anyone right now. The currents will be worse than lethal.*

14.
Impact

The further Xanthe was pulled out, the stronger the currents seemed to become. They sucked at her exhausted limbs, twisting her this way and that until she felt as helpless as a rag doll. She tried to dodge the endless trail of rubbish eddying and swirling towards her, but it was no use – the currents had her in their grasp and her flesh was soon smarting with cuts and bruises.

And then a far greater force struck her – a vast, relentless tide, ripping her rucksack off her back and sweeping her downstream.

Panic overwhelmed her. She squeezed her eyes shut and cradled her head in her hands. Another few moments and she would surely crash into one of the larger pieces of debris and be knocked unconscious.

Then the tide would hurl her on towards the next obstacle, then the next and the next, until it had battered all the life from her and there would be nothing left for it to do but spew her out into the sea.

The impact, when it came, seemed to crush every bone in her body. Fireworks of pain shot through her as she waited for the tide to sweep her on … but the moment never arrived. Behind her closed eyelids she could see little explosions of white light and for a second she wondered whether she was already dead. But that didn't make sense. Dead people couldn't think, could they? And they couldn't feel pain, either.

Slowly, she uncurled her hands from round her head and opened her eyes. She had smashed into something huge – something which seemed to be made out of a stony substance: concrete, perhaps.

For a while she kept quite still, pressed like a limpet against the strange object that had saved her from the sweeping tide. Then, after a few minutes had passed, she reached her hand above her head and began to drag herself up it.

Her injured shin scuffed against the stone, but she ignored the pain and pulled herself higher and higher until at last she saw a patch of dappled light not far above her.

Xanthe scaled the final metre and broke the

surface of the water. She took a steadying breath of air, then gazed about. She was clinging to a huge mound of mud-coated concrete in the middle of the river; some distance to her right she could see an identical concrete mound; to either side of her were the two banks and all around her surged the choppy waters of the Thames.

She looked up … and blinked. Above her was something so extraordinary she thought for a moment she must be dreaming. She appeared to be staring at some kind of fairytale castle: a pair of tall towers, linked near the top by a couple of fancy walkways and decorated with turrets and spires. Flags flew from the walkways and each tower was studded with tiny windows that glinted in the January sunshine.

And then she realized what it was. She'd seen it countless times before — and the last time was from the riverbank just now, before Donna had blindfolded her.

The tide had hurled her straight into the base of Tower Bridge.

Xanthe hauled herself round the mound of concrete, gritting her teeth against the pain in her shin. If she could just get to the other side of it, she might escape the main pull of the tide and be able to swim to safety. It wasn't *that* far to the riverbank – and at least now she could see where she was heading.

She stretched out her arm and inched a little further round the bottom of the bridge. The next moment a bolt of white heat was shooting through her, knocking her back under the water. Her heart thundered against her chest. She'd recognize that feeling anywhere. It was the same sensation she had felt beside the boathouse, after Donna had chased her out of the lake. She clearly hadn't escaped the witches yet – she was being hexed.

Reaching her hand behind her back, she checked the pocket of her jeans for her locket. Thank goodness it was still there.

She clung to the base of the bridge. Whatever else she did, she mustn't lose contact with it. She tried to calm herself. The Hexing Witches must have been keeping an eye on her, and seen her coming up from the river. She could still feel the heat from the hex, but it wasn't so intense now; if she stayed underwater she would probably be OK.

Then again, staying down here wouldn't actually achieve anything, would it? She'd be running away from the one chance she had to do something about the situation. It'd be a massive risk, but by putting her head above water and focusing on the witches, she might be able to save more than just herself.

Without stopping to think any further, Xanthe came back up to the heaving surface and turned to face the north bank of the river. Some way upstream, she could see the little group of abandoned barges, and standing on one of them were the Hexing Witches, a row of figures clinging on to the boat as it lurched from side to side. Just above them, a helicopter circled low – they had clearly been spotted.

She shrank back against the concrete base of the bridge as another hex struck her – and then another. What on earth did she think she was doing? She had to be completely mad. The last time she'd tried to defend herself against a Hexing Witch, there had been only one of them. This time there were about a dozen. And she was weaker than she'd been when it had happened before, much weaker – her battle with the tide and the wound to her leg had made sure of that.

The heat from a fourth hex seared through her, electrifying her entire body. But this time she held fast, gripping on to the base of the bridge for support and forcing herself to focus on the line of witches. She concentrated on them with every ounce of her strength, allowing only the thoughts that mattered to fill her brain. She was the only one who could stop them. She *had* to do it. The number of people who would be killed if the city flooded didn't bear thinking about.

Inside the pocket of her jeans, her locket was becoming warm, and above the choppy waters of the Thames there appeared a single, tiny flame. Xanthe continued to stare at the witches, murmuring the words she had intoned when she had faced Donna down at the boathouse. "I am Xanthe Fox," she whispered. "I am a True Witch."

Her gaze grew stronger, and the flame started to move towards the line of witches. It travelled slowly at first, then gathered speed, a weird orange beacon hovering over the river.

Not far from the banks it burst into a wall of fire – and the barge ignited. A few seconds later the barges on either side of it caught alight, sending an enormous plume of smoke into the air.

Xanthe relaxed her focus, allowing herself a few seconds to take in the scene: the towering blaze; the helicopter hovering above the haze of thick black smoke; the figures running in every direction. A few of them even seemed to be throwing themselves into the water.

A wave of triumph surged through her, followed almost immediately by a feeling of sickness. She'd stopped the witches in their tracks – but at what cost? Was it possible she'd *killed* some of them?

She turned her back on the scene, trying to wipe the question from her brain. She mustn't think like that. Those Hexing Witches had been trying to flood London. They wouldn't have paused to consider how many people *they* might kill.

Xanthe clung to the base of the bridge, her body shaking. For now, everyone's attention would be on the burning barges, but it wouldn't be long before somebody saw her and raised the alarm. She ducked under the water and pulled herself round the mound of concrete, away from the main sweep of the tide. Was it her imagination, or was its pull already less vicious? She set off towards the bank, battling against the currents.

Halfway there, she surfaced to check on her position. The air was thick with the noise of sirens and helicopters, and out of the corner of her eye she could see flames still leaping from the barges. Ahead of her were the railings of the north bank.

And there was something else, too – just beyond the railings. Some*one* else: an old woman in a mushroom-brown duffel coat and a black beret.

For a terrible moment Xanthe thought that one of the Hexing Witches must have jumped off the barge before it had caught fire and raced up to the bridge to meet her – but then she saw that the woman was beckoning to her and smiling.

"You must be Xanthe!" called the old lady. "I'm Peggy, in case you hadn't realized." She waited until Xanthe had swum the final distance to the bank, then reached out and helped her over the railings. "You've no idea how glad I am to see you!"

15.
Rescue

Peggy enveloped Xanthe in a huge hug.

"Are you all right?" she exclaimed. "I came as quickly as I could. Oh, Xanthe – your great-grandmother is going to be *so* proud of you!"

Xanthe freed herself from the old lady's embrace and leaned against the railings, gasping for breath.

"What's happened to the water level?" she panted, peering down at the Thames. "Are the banks definitely going to hold?"

Peggy unbuttoned her duffel coat and draped it round Xanthe's shoulders. "I'm sure they are. I only got here a minute ago, but even in that time the river's gone down a good few inches."

"But – but how did you know where to come?" asked Xanthe. "How did you—" She broke off as her legs suddenly gave way beneath her and she slumped to the ground.

"Oh, you poor thing!" cried Peggy, kneeling down beside her. "You must be completely shattered!" She glanced around. "Look, I've got lots of questions to ask you, too, but let's leave all that for now. We could do with finding some cover while you have a bit of a rest and we sort ourselves out." She pointed to a nearby archway. "D'you think you could make it over there if I helped you?"

Xanthe pulled herself upright and, leaning on Peggy's arm, limped towards the shelter of the archway.

"What've you done to your leg?" asked Peggy, once they were sitting down inside. She frowned at Xanthe's bloodstained jeans.

"I cut myself on a sheet of metal in the river," murmured Xanthe. Now she was out of the water, the cold was starting to seep into her bones and she couldn't stop her teeth from chattering. "I'll be OK in a minute. I'm just exhausted from all that concentrating and the pull of the tide. It ripped my rucksack off my back. And my mobile's gone, too. It must have fallen out of my hoodie."

Peggy gazed at her, a glazed expression on her face. "What you did was amazing, Xanthe. Surviving the tide, and dealing with the Hexing Witches.

Seeing that flame move over the water towards the barge was incredible."

"So you witnessed the whole thing?"

Peggy nodded. "I got there a few moments before it happened."

Xanthe frowned. "But you still haven't explained how you knew where to find me."

"You told me where to find you."

"*Told* you?"

"Yes. Remember that last conversation we had before your phone cut out? You said you were on Gregory Street, and that you reckoned you were nearly at your destination. So when I finally managed to get a taxi, all I had to do was tell the driver to step on it." Peggy snorted. "Not that he was too keen to take me when I told him where we were heading. But he soon changed his tune when I offered to pay triple fare. He even agreed to wait for me."

Xanthe listened in silence.

"When we arrived I made straight for the river," went on Peggy. "That's where I guessed all the action would be. I was nearly there when I heard shouting, so I crept forward and saw a line of women standing on a barge and pointing down at the water. '*The girl's jumped in!*' one of them was yelling. '*The True Witch has jumped into the river!*'"

She ran her hand over her forehead. "You can't

imagine how I felt then. I tried to think straight, but I just couldn't work out what to do for the best. There was no point in me leaping in after you – I might be a witch, but I'm also very nearly eighty. I wouldn't have stood a chance in that whirlpool of a river. I was all set to ring the emergency services when the Hexing Witches started shouting again, this time about someone clinging to the bottom of Tower Bridge. A moment later they were shooting hexes across the water, and before I had a chance to react, you were zapping them back with fire."

"Do you reckon some of them might have been burned alive?" asked Xanthe. She clenched her jaw as the wave of sickness she had felt earlier engulfed her once again.

Peggy squeezed her arm. "I don't know," she said. "I didn't hang around long enough to find out. All I can be sure of is that young schoolmate of yours escaped the blaze. I saw a girl of about your age running from the scene just before the barge went up in flames."

Xanthe felt herself relax a little. She hated Donna with every atom of her body, but she didn't want her *dead*. That would definitely be a step too far.

"Now it's your turn," said Peggy. "I want to know exactly what happened to you. What made you throw yourself into the Thames, for heaven's sake?"

"I didn't have much choice," said Xanthe. "As soon as we got to the witches' headquarters they all came running out towards me. Donna had lured me there, you see – she'd set me up right from the start." Peggy's eyes widened. "They dragged me down to the river and Donna blindfolded me and tied my hands behind my back with a piece of rope. Then she tried to take my locket off me, and I figured my only hope of escape was to jump into the water. Plus, of course, I thought I might stand a better chance of reversing the hexes that way." She pulled her locket out of the back pocket of her jeans and ran her fingers over its smooth silver casing.

"Oh!" breathed Peggy, staring down at it. "It's even more beautiful than I remember! I've seen it before, of course, round Alice's neck, but I've never actually touched it." She held out her hand. "May I?"

"Of course," said Xanthe, passing it to Peggy. "It's still warm from all that reverse hexing. I expect the moonstone is as well."

Peggy opened the locket and caressed the oval of moonstone inside.

"You're right," she said. "It is. How absolutely incredible." She sighed. "It's amazing to think this belonged to Ethelfreda. To the first in your line of True Witches. What a wonderful thing to inherit. All I got was a plain old ring from *my* ancestor."

She closed the casing and gave the locket back to Xanthe. "So what happened when you were in the Thames?" she asked.

"I managed to free myself from the rope and the blindfold," said Xanthe. "And then I tried to swim to safety. But the currents kept pulling me out into the middle of the river, and the next thing I knew, the tide was sweeping me downstream and hurling me into Tower Bridge. I think you can probably guess the rest." She squeezed the locket. "You haven't told me what you did once the barge had caught fire. How did you get over here?"

"Well, I knew it wouldn't be long before the place was teeming with emergency services," said Peggy. "And in any case, I wanted to get to *you*. So I hotfooted it back to the taxi and asked the driver to take me as close to Tower Bridge as he could. I only just caught him in time, mind you. He was about to drive away – he'd seen the smoke from the barge and was wondering what on earth was going on."

"Did he ask you whether you knew anything about the fire?"

"Not exactly. But he did give me a funny look. I got him to drop me near the bridge and told him to wait a couple of streets down till needed him again. I think he was finding it all rather an adventure."

"And he's still waiting there?"

"I certainly hope so," said Peggy. "In fact, if you've had enough of a rest, I think we should probably get out of here and go and find him. You must come back to my house for a while, so I can clean up that leg of yours. Then you can have a shower and I'll make you something to eat before you head back to the station."

Something stirred in the depths of Xanthe's brain. Something that had nothing to do with hexes or burning barges or river levels. It was a moment before she realized what it was.

Her date with Saul! She'd forgotten all about it!

"No, no!" she cried, stumbling to her feet. "I mean, it's really kind of you and everything, but I've got to get to Victoria *now*! I need to get home before ... before..." She glanced down at her watch, then frowned. It had stopped at a little after eleven o'clock – almost certainly the time she had leaped into the water.

Peggy smiled. "Stop panicking! It's only just gone twelve. We don't have to be long at my place. I'll have you on a train by two o'clock at the latest, I promise. That'll give you bags of time to get home. Your parents won't suspect a thing."

Xanthe ran her fingers through her hair. "But the trains were all over the place earlier on, and it'll probably take ages for them to get back to normal." She flushed. "And anyway, it's not my parents I'm worried about. I – well, I'm meeting someone after school. A boy in my class. I've already stood him up once this week, and I can't let him down again."

Peggy raised her eyebrows. "Oh, I *see!*" she said. "Well, you definitely can't be late for *that*." She considered for a moment. "I'll tell you what – how about we pick up some first-aid stuff in the chemist at Victoria? And if there's time, we'll buy you some new clothes, too – there should be a couple of shops in the concourse. The ones you're wearing might as well be binned. They're filthy and sopping wet, and they smell pretty bad, too. Riverwater wouldn't be my first choice of perfume for a hot date."

Xanthe blushed an even deeper shade of red. The thought that her meeting with Saul might end up as a hot date made her stomach turn to jelly.

"Thanks, Peggy," she murmured. "Thanks for being so understanding."

Together they made their way to where the taxi was waiting.

As they approached, the driver leaned out of the window and waved. "At last!" he shouted. "I'd almost given up on you!" He grinned. "Not that I've had a boring time or anything. I've had the radio on, and it's been non-stop action. The emergency services are trying to put out that fire we saw earlier. Seems a group of nutters were messing about on a barge and managed to set light to it."

Xanthe's lips twitched, but she said nothing.

"And the water level's dropped almost back to normal, too," went on the driver. "The authorities can't explain it, and I can't say as I can, either." He shook his head in disbelief. "Anyway, the city can get back to business as usual — that's all that matters."

"Well, I never," said Peggy, stooping to climb into the taxi. "The things that happen in London, hey? Whoever would have thought it!"

Xanthe got in after her, careful to keep Peggy's duffel coat wrapped tightly round her. At least her hair was so short it had already dried.

The driver turned and winked at her. "Your granny, I take it?" he said in a stage whisper. "Bit scary, isn't she? I wouldn't want to get on the wrong side of her."

Xanthe opened her mouth to correct him, then shut it again. What was the point in trying to explain? Much better to let him draw his own conclusions about who they were and what they'd been doing. Whatever he came up with, it would be far less extraordinary than the truth.

"Where to this time?" asked the driver.

Peggy leaned forward. "Victoria Station, please," she said. "And as fast as you can. This young lady has an appointment she can't afford to miss."

16.
The Kiss

Xanthe stood at the end of the carriage, squashed between a young man in a leather jacket and a group of women. It didn't look like she was ever going to get a seat.

She'd had to wait ages for a train at Victoria, and when at last a service to Milchester had been announced, it seemed the whole world had rushed towards the platform with her, elbowing past one another in an effort to get onboard.

She glanced down at the new watch Peggy had insisted on buying her at the station and frowned. Nearly three o'clock already. She'd be lucky to make it back in time for her date with Saul. They were only about twenty minutes away from Milchester, but the train was crawling along at a snail's pace.

Xanthe drummed her fingers against her thigh, wishing she still had Peggy with her for company. The old lady would have managed to keep her calm however slowly the train was going. She'd been brilliant right up to the very last moment, when she'd thrown her arms round her for a final hug. As soon as the taxi had pulled up outside Victoria, she had dashed into a chemist for a first-aid kit, then sat her down in a nearby photo booth while she bandaged up her shin. After that she'd taken her to a clothes shop and told her to choose whatever she fancied. Ten minutes later Xanthe had found herself inside one of the changing rooms, pulling on a gorgeous new top and some seriously cool jeans. Peggy had even treated her to a new pair of trainers. "A reward for saving London," she had whispered through the door.

Xanthe looked out of the train window and allowed herself a small smile. The old lady really had thought of everything. Just as they were saying goodbye, she had pressed a tiny bottle of perfume into her hands and told her to use it to freshen up on the journey. She'd done as she was told and sprayed a bit behind her ears, but more out of a sense of duty than anything else. It was way too flowery for her liking, though it was probably better than smelling of riverwater.

Peggy had also insisted on handing over her

mobile in case of emergencies, saying she could have it back the weekend after next, when she'd promised to come up to Milchester and have tea with her and Grandma Alice. It would be a real treat, she'd said.

Xanthe gazed out at the countryside and thought of her great-grandmother lying in hospital. It was going to be such a relief to blurt it all out to her. Especially when she would have to tell everyone else a pack of lies.

She sighed to herself. Life had got so complicated. Grace and Saul were under the impression she'd been ill in bed all day, and her mother thought she'd been at school – she'd have to sneak back to Grandma Alice's later on and change into her school uniform before heading home. There was no way she was going to risk Mum seeing her dressed in completely new clothes. She'd have to hide them away for a few days and say she'd bought them on a shopping trip with Grace at the weekend. And what about the wound to her shin? And the fact she'd lost her mobile? She was going to have to think of some seriously good excuses.

Her ears pricked up as the lady beside her started talking to one of her companions.

"It doesn't make sense, does it?" she said. "I mean, one minute the water level's rising like mad, and the next it's almost back to normal – and with no explanation whatsoever. Oh, and did you know there was a fire near Tower Bridge, too?"

"I heard," replied her friend. "I was checking the news updates on my phone earlier on and they reckon three women died in the incident. Apparently they were very badly burned." She shook her head. "I just don't understand what they were doing down there in the first place. There were enough warnings to stay away."

Xanthe shuddered. The knowledge that some of the Hexing Witches had definitely died in the blaze made her stomach churn. What did that make her exactly? A *murderer*? She gave herself a shake. She mustn't think like that. If she hadn't summoned fire and forced the witches to stop their hexing, most of London would have been flooded by now, and how many people would have been killed or injured *then*? At least she knew Donna had escaped. She was probably cowering in some abandoned shop or warehouse, wishing she'd never got involved in the first place. Or she might even be on this train. Either way, she wasn't likely to cause her much bother at the moment.

"There's all sorts of stories flying around," went on the first lady. "There's one report of a kid seen in the water beside Tower Bridge, but that's *got* to be a hoax. No one would have survived in the Thames today. Not even for a minute."

Xanthe turned away and switched on Peggy's phone, racking her brains to remember Grace's number. The bell for the end of school should have gone by now, and she'd give anything to exchange a few nice, ordinary texts with her friend.

Borrowing a spare phone to text you, she keyed into Peggy's mobile. *Have lost mine. Have you had a good day?*

Grace's reply came back almost at once.

LOST IT?! How did you manage that?! Does that mean you didn't pick up the message I left you at lunchtime?

Xanthe hesitated. If there was one thing she hated more than anything else, it was lying to Grace.

Long story, she wrote back, playing for time. *What did your message say?*

Oh, it was about something funny that happened in English, that's all.

Xanthe's fingers flew over Peggy's mobile. *Well??? Don't keep me in suspense!*

Miss Ambrose moved on to another scene in Macbeth, replied Grace. *And you'll never guess who she chose to play Lady Macbeth!*

Who?

Kelly, of course! How fitting is that?!

A grin spread across Xanthe's face. *Excellent!* she texted back. *Talk about typecasting!*

The mobile beeped with another message.

Are you still meeting Saul this afternoon?

Xanthe glanced out of the window again. They were passing the industrial estate on the outskirts of Milchester, and in the distance she could see the park and a tiny section of the lake. They couldn't be more than a couple of minutes away at most.

On my way there now, she replied. *Ring you later!*

She switched off the phone and began to move towards the doors. It looked like she might just make it after all.

"I'd nearly given up hope!" exclaimed Saul, giving Xanthe a shy smile as she stood gasping for breath beside him.

Xanthe flapped one hand in front of her in an effort to cool down. Just before the train had got to the station, it had stopped for almost five minutes, and she'd had to run like crazy to make it in time. Shooting pains were rocketing up her wounded shin and her entire body felt like it was burning up.

"Have you sprinted the whole way here?" said Saul. "I thought you were supposed to be *ill*."

Xanthe pushed her hair off her forehead and groaned to herself. She couldn't believe she was turning up to her first ever date looking like a beetroot. And smelling of a combination of sweat, dirty water and flowers, too.

"I'm ... not ... that ... bad!" she puffed. "I stayed in bed all morning but I started to feel better around lunchtime." She straightened her new top and smoothed down her jeans. "I lost track of time, that's all."

"Well, you only needed to text me," said Saul. "I would have waited." He peered at her more closely. "Hey, how did you get that bruise above your eye?"

Xanthe hesitated. She'd hadn't even noticed she *had* a bruise above her eye. Compared with the wound to her shin, her other cuts and bruises didn't count for anything. But she could hardly say that to Saul.

"I – er – banged into a door, that's all," she said. She cleared her throat. "So, where're we going, then? Have you got any ideas?"

The shy expression returned to Saul's face. "Well," he said, "I wondered whether you'd like to try out that new coffee place that's opened in the shopping centre. Or else there's the ice-cream parlour. But it might be a bit cold for that."

Xanthe thought for a moment. There *was* somewhere she wanted to go. Somewhere she hadn't been to for quite some time, and which she could be pretty sure was absolutely safe now.

"D'you know what?" she said. "If it's OK with you, I'd like to go down to the park. I know I told you before I wasn't too keen, and I realize it's only January, but it's so lovely and sunny, it seems a shame to be indoors."

"But what about your mum and dad? I thought they didn't want you going there."

Xanthe rolled her eyes.

"Oh, you know what parents are like," she said. "Forever fussing." She grinned. "Come on, they don't need to know where we've been, do they?"

Saul laughed. "OK, then," he said. "As you say, it's a nice day, and anyway, I want to see for myself what it looks like down there. I've only seen the pictures in the paper."

They set off towards the park in silence. Xanthe racked her brain for something to say, but now they'd decided where to go, she couldn't think of a single sensible topic of conversation.

As they neared the entrance, Xanthe's heart sank – the park was swarming with visitors. Of course! It had only reopened at the start of the week; it was bound to be full of people anxious to get a look at the burned-out remains of the boathouse – and they'd probably all be gossiping about it, too. It was hardly the best choice of venue. Still, she wasn't going to

161

make a fuss. She'd just have to make the best of it.

"D'you fancy a drink?" asked Saul, making for the café.

Xanthe shook her head. "I'm OK, thanks." The last thing she wanted to do right now was bump into the lady she'd sat opposite on the train this morning. "Let's go for a walk instead."

Saul gestured towards the space beyond the bandstand where the thicket of trees had once stood. "Why don't we see how bad the damage is?"

They passed the swings and the bandstand and hurried on in the direction of the lake. Not far off a group of people had gathered next to a makeshift barrier of red-and-white-striped plastic; they were talking and pointing towards the boathouse.

Saul let out a low whistle as they drew near. "It's even worse than it looked in the photos!" he exclaimed. "There's almost nothing left of the boathouse, and loads of the trees have gone, too."

Xanthe said nothing. She could still recall quite clearly the scene as it had been when it was on fire. Flames had leaped into the wintry dusk; ash had showered down around her; the whole place had been alive with movement and colour. Now all that was left were the blackened remains of the boathouse and a few miserable-looking tree stumps.

Saul glanced across at her and touched her lightly

on the arm. "It could have been a lot worse, you know," he said. "At least no one was hurt. Come on, let's head over to the lake. We can get round this way, I think."

Xanthe followed him until they found themselves on one of the narrow footpaths leading towards the lake. They walked side by side, neither of them saying a word. Once or twice Xanthe felt Saul's hand brush against hers, and a shiver ran up her spine.

They stopped beside the lake and stared out at the glittering water.

"D'you remember coming down here last summer with me and Grace?" asked Saul. "Hiring that boat and nearly capsizing it?"

Xanthe nodded. "It was awesome." She gave him a nudge. "Except it was you doing all the capsizing. Grace and I were sitting perfectly still."

Saul turned to her and grinned. "Whatever. I just know it was brilliant fun." He dropped his gaze. "I – I think about that day a lot, you know."

"Really?" murmured Xanthe. "I thought it was just me who did that."

Saul sighed. "The trouble with you, Xanthe Fox," he said, "is that you haven't got a clue how special you are."

He moved towards her – and, tilting his head, pressed his lips against hers.

Xanthe closed her eyes, wishing it would last forever. It was happening. It was actually happening. The moment she'd hardly dared dream of.

Saul pulled away at last. "Believe me now?" He gently traced his finger over the bruise above her eye. "Believe me that you're special?"

"OK," she said. "I believe you. Just this once."

"And you'll go out with me?"

Xanthe looked back at him, her heart exploding inside her chest.

"Of course I will," she said. She took his hands in hers and smiled. "I'd like nothing better."

Also available:

Journey back to the very beginning…

Xanthe stared down at the test paper and gasped. A thick line had been slashed across it, and at the bottom, in her own handwriting, were the words, Miss Pimm's maths class stinks.

Xanthe can't wait to turn thirteen, but as her birthday nears, her world starts to fall apart. Set up at school, it seems her age-old enemy, Kelly, is making trouble for her. With her friends deserting her, and mysterious glowing Xs appearing in front of her eyes, Xanthe turns to her great-grandmother for help. But what the old lady tells her will change Xanthe's life forever…

Harriet Goodwin

GRAVENHUNGER

Unlock the ghostly secret...

*Phoenix gasped. How could she
have kept a place like this a secret? It was
huge. Four storeys of dark grey stone glowering down
at them through a multitude of mullioned windows.*

*... The sun had disappeared behind a
dense bank of cloud – and above the towering
chimneys of Gravenhunger Manor a thin
grey rain was falling.*

Gravenhunger Manor isn't the only
secret Phoenix's mother took with her to the
grave. Something terrible happened at the house
during her childhood, something for which she
never forgave herself. Phoenix is determined to
uncover the truth, but as he begins to dig up the
past, he finds himself in mortal danger...

Turn the page to read an
exciting extract...

1.
Elvira's Letter

"No way!" said Phoenix, glaring at his father across the kitchen table. "I'm not going. Not for the whole of the summer holidays. And not with *Rose*!"

Dr Wainwright sighed. He put down his knife and fork and leaned back in his chair.

"What's wrong with Rose? She was nice enough to you at the funeral, wasn't she?"

Phoenix dropped his gaze.

"Of course she was nice to me at the funeral," he muttered. "Everyone was. But that doesn't mean I want to go on holiday with her! Six weeks, Dad! With a girl I hardly know! What on earth were you thinking?"

"I was partly thinking of your cousin, actually," said Dr Wainwright.

He ran his fingers through his greying hair.

"Rose has just come back from four years abroad. I don't suppose she's made many friends at her new school yet, so I thought she might like to come on holiday with us."

Phoenix scowled.

"But why couldn't I have asked one of my mates from school? Jake or Sam, maybe?" He pushed his plate to one side. "And what's with all this going away business, anyway? We never go on holiday. Never. Why change things now? And why spring it on me at the last minute?"

His father raised his eyebrows. "Because I knew you'd kick up one almighty great fuss," he said. "Exactly like you're doing now."

Phoenix flushed and fumbled in his pocket for a piece of chewing gum.

"Look," his father went on. "You're right, we never go on holiday. You know Mum couldn't stand being away from home. But – well, things are different now. And I thought a proper break would do us good." He glanced at his son's pale face. "Goodness knows we could do with one after the year we've had."

There was a long silence.

"So what's this place like, anyway?" said Phoenix at last. "What did you say it was called again?"

"Gravenhunger Manor. It's on the south coast.

A couple of miles outside the village of Gravenhunger."

Phoenix rolled his eyes.

"Honestly, Dad. First holiday we've ever been on and you go and choose some old place by the sea I've never even heard of. Why couldn't we have gone abroad? Why couldn't we have gone somewhere *interesting*?"

"You know we can't afford that sort of holiday," replied his father. "Especially since the university cut back on my teaching hours. Things aren't easy at the moment, Phoenix. Besides, I think you'll like where we're going. Gravenhunger Manor must have been very grand in its day. The house is huge and so are the grounds. There's a big garden at the back and a pine forest surrounding the whole thing, and a river beyond the trees. It's got something about it. Something unusual. Something different."

"Yeah?" said Phoenix. "And how would you know that?" He frowned suddenly. "You've been there before, haven't you?"

Dr Wainwright shifted in his seat. He opened his mouth to speak, then shut it again.

Phoenix folded his arms, his eyes now fixed upon his father.

"Come on, Dad. There's something you're not telling me, isn't there?"

His father cleared his throat. "There *is* something I

need to tell you about Gravenhunger Manor. But…"

"But what?"

"It's a bit tricky, that's all. I was going to leave it till we were on our way down there tomorrow. I thought the journey would give us a chance for a good long chat before Rose arrives."

"Can't you tell me now?"

"The last thing I want to do is stir things up for you, Phoenix…"

"Dad! Stop treating me like a little kid! I'm nearly thirteen, in case you'd forgotten."

Dr Wainwright rested his elbows on the table and met his son's gaze.

"All right," he said. "You win. I'll tell you what all this is about."

He took off his glasses and rubbed his eyes.

"This place we're going to," he said, "this house in the middle of nowhere. It – it belonged to your mother. Gravenhunger Manor belonged to her."

"To *Mum*?"

Phoenix gaped at his father.

"But she never said anything. She never even mentioned it."

"No, not to you – and not to me either."

"You're saying you didn't know anything about it?"

Dr Wainwright replaced his glasses and shook

his head. "Nothing at all," he said. "Not until the solicitor's papers landed on my desk back in February. It was just as much a surprise to me then as it is to you now."

"But *why* didn't she say anything? Did she leave you some sort of an explanation?"

His father glanced away. He picked up his fork and began to push his unfinished food around the plate.

"Not really," he said. "All I know is that Gravenhunger Manor was bought by your mother's parents many years ago. It seems they lived there for a short time when your mum was a child. For whatever reason the house was never sold when they moved on – so when your grandparents died, it was passed down to your mother."

"And now it's yours?"

"That's right. Which is why I thought it'd be a good idea to go down there this summer and take a proper look at it."

"But I still don't understand," said Phoenix. "Why would Mum keep something like that secret?"

Dr Wainwright got up from the table. "I'm afraid it's all a bit of a mystery," he said, gathering up the plates and carrying them over to the worktop. "But I expect she had her reasons."

He stood there for a moment, his back to his son.

"Your mother was quite a complicated person, you know."

"And what's that supposed to mean?" demanded Phoenix.

His father turned round to face him. "Don't get me wrong," he said. "She was a wonderful mother and she loved you with all her heart. But she was a woman of secrets. She always held herself back. Not so much from you, perhaps. But certainly from me."

A shadow passed across his face.

"Just think about how long she kept her illness from us both. She knew how to keep things quiet. And it looks like it was the same with this house. If she had some reason not to tell us about it, then we just have to respect that. I'm not about to start raking things up. There's no point. We have to look forward now, you and I. Find a way to start again."

Phoenix looked away.

A woman of secrets. It was weird hearing Dad talk about Mum like that. It didn't seem right.

He pictured the little silver angel, zipped inside his blazer pocket upstairs.

That had been a sort of secret too, now he came to think about it. But at least it was one Mum had chosen to share with him.

She had given him the angel the day before she died. He'd never seen it before, but it clearly meant the world to her. She'd put it into his hands, her dark eyes searching his face, and asked him to keep it safe.

And so he had taken it, fighting back the tears and trying not to look too hard at the grey face on the pillow before him. Since that day he had carried it with him everywhere, knowing neither how nor why it soothed him, knowing only that it was his special link with her, and that he couldn't be without it. It wasn't exactly cool to own an angel, but he was never going to let it go.

Also available:

The Boy Who Fell Down Exit 43

Harriet Goodwin

*For a millionth of a second the car grazed the
drenched moorland. If it had come down on any other
patch of ground Finn would simply have been another
statistic. Death by dangerous driving. But the car hit
the surface of the Earth at Exit 43. … And at that
moment, though no one yet knew it, the entire future
of the Underworld changed course.*

Finn Oliver knows he'll never come to terms with
his father's death, but joy-riding over the moors in his
mum's beat-up old car is a quick fix of freedom and
forgetting. Until the accident happens and Finn finds
himself hurtling through the wafer-thin divide between
the worlds of the living and the dead…

Harriet Goodwin read medieval English
at Oxford University before training as a
professional singer. After the birth of her
fourth child she had a vivid dream about a
boy who fell through the surface of the
Earth into a ghostly Underworld – and
this became the setting for her first
novel, *The Boy Who Fell Down Exit 43*.
She lives in Staffordshire
with her family.

**For more
about the author,
visit her website:**

www.harrietgoodwinbooks.com